The Voice

The Voice

Paul Fitzgerald and Elizabeth Gould

To order additional copies of this book, contact:
Xlibris Corporation
1-888-7-XLIBRIS
www.Xlibris.com
Orders@Xlibris.com

Contents

L

PREFACE

"Addicted to dreams and visions," was how the nineteenth century historians that rediscovered his work described Geraldus Cambrensis, (Gerald de Barry), author of the original twelfth century eyewitness accounts of the invasion of Ireland. When my wife Liz and I set out to write a story called The Voice ten years ago we never considered that the devoutly religious Cambrensis or his mystical dreams had any meaning to us.

We were budding, hard-edged truth seekers—the first Americans to get a film crew into Soviet occupied Kabul after the invasion of Afghanistan in 1979. Following the events closely, we had seen through the veil of the greatest CIA effort since Vietnam, arranged to fly into the heart of the Evil Empire's war machine and returned with a story for CBS News that was in stark contrast to the barrage of reports we'd seen of the war.

Here was an impoverished nation struggling to survive its own feudal past, crushed by the whims and ideals of two imperial fathers, the U.S. and Soviet Union, bent on proving their own righteousness. Ours was a complex and charged story, so powerful Oliver Stone eventually optioned the film rights.

But Afghanistan was always more than met the eye. Over the years we watched with deep sadness at the endless progression of the war, suspecting there were deeper reasons for the countless failures to achieve a peace but always finding them elusive. Meanwhile the war worsened, spreading chaos to other countries in the region.

Unknown to all but a handful of people, a nuclear war was narrowly averted in 1990 between India and Pakistan and the situation in the region continues to disintegrate to this day. What could possibly have motivated the instigators of this war to bring us to the edge of Armageddon on the eve of the millennium?

After years of struggling with that impossible story, the Voice was to be our attempt to escape the madness of that war. Inspired by Joseph Campbell's Power of Myth we would plunge into a story of myth and legend, leaving the world of geopolitics and hard-edged journalism behind. But instead of an escape, our search began to reveal deeper, far reaching motives for the events that modern journalism only touches on. And in time, we began a thoroughly mystical journey that led us—through dreams and coincidence—to find our personal connection to these historical events as well. It began suddenly in 1991, the tenth anniversary year of our first trip to Afghanistan when our daughter Alissa awoke, having dreamed of my deceased father.

Accompanied by a strange man and wearing a peculiar bell bottomed plaid suit and a funny matching hat, the man claimed to be a friend of my father and when my daughter questioned his age he laughed and told her he was eight hundred years old. Over the years I had heard many tales of the Fitzgerald family and their eight-hundred year old conquest of Ireland under the Earl of Pembroke, Strongbow. I also knew that my branch of the family was somehow connected to them. But the coming of Alissa's dream seemed an omen I couldn't ignore and I immediately set out to find whether this mysterious visitor might be a connection I was looking for.

We started by combing the library for clues and within days Liz had managed to find a hundred-year-old copy of Cambrensis' account hidden in the Boston Public Library. As a prelate educated in the finest schools on the continent and private tutor to Henry II's son Prince John, Geraldus Cambrensis—as he was known—provided a unique vantage on the controversial invasion, recording and nuancing an already intriguing story with his own back-channel knowledge and inside information hot from the English court. But as a Fitzgerald, grandson of Gerald of Windsor and the famous Nesta, a Tudor Princess whose lineage traced back to the mythical Celtic court of Arthur—Cambrensis offered much more than the usual scribe's-eye view. What Cambrensis offered was "prophecy" on the future of his boss, King Henry II, his own family, the Fitzgeralds and the fate of the "West" at the end of this millennium.

He had gone to the great trouble of finding the only original copy of the legendary Merlin's prophecies because "the rough and unvarnished simplicity of the older idiom was the only true friend of truth," and he had used his dreams and visions to guide him to where that truth was hidden. It was a powerful document and reading it was like gazing into a crystal whose facets reflected not only a mystical view of history, but my own family's role in it.

It was all there, the dream, the visions, the predictions recorded by one of the most acknowledged voices of the twelfth century in a language so contemporary it read like it had been written yesterday. Just as I had done in Afghanistan, I recognized Cambrensis' desire to chronicle an historical event and identified with the difficulty of what he was trying to reveal.

I also saw in his account the slow and steady mystical awakening that changed him from being a strict Catholic prelate into a Merlin-like prophet and I sensed in that something important for me. He understood that there were essential meanings missing from our understanding of history and our place in it, meanings that Western thought had filtered out. He understood that whether pagan or Christian, there were secrets to our simultaneous existence in other realms of reality and that only by listening to our dreams could we fully understand what was in store for us.

Cambrensis had intended to put them all in a separate book and call it the "Prophetic history of Ireland." But in the end he had suppressed them, fearing that "the prophecies must wait until the right time has arrived."

When I read those words, written by candlelight on a piece of parchment eight hundred years before my time, a voice called out to me that the "right time" was now. I believed that somehow, the eight hundred year old visitor to my daughter's dream was a messenger. But I had no idea at the time what that message was, or in the end, the sacrifices it would require of me to find it. But so, I began.

Standing on this side of the experience seven years later, I look back at that time with very different eyes. The suspicions that had prompted me to feel that "things were not as they seemed," having been realized beyond my wildest imaginings. Over these last seven years, new dimensions of reality have presented themselves, mythic dreams have become reality and a new multi-dimensional universe has been opened and explored. It almost seems too much to believe and all of it might have remained unwritten and confined to our personal dream world had it not been for the interest of Oliver Stone. Having gone to him with a concept for the Voice after the movie JFK we found Stone to have an avid interest in the power of dreams, having named his own company IXTLAN after a Carlos Casteneda book on the subject.

But Stone's interest was for Afghanistan and from the moment we met, our dreams seemed to slip into mythic overdrive. Materializing with a nearly three-dimensional holographic quality, Liz found herself nightly in elaborate settings, Greek Temples, French Chateaus. There, in shimmering Versailles-like palaces of light, Oliver would listen to her hopes and dreams and tell her of his plans to make her dreams come true. My dreams assumed a more business-like quality, meeting Oliver in production somewhere in Afghanistan, discussing the risks of the adventure. The dreams even assumed the practical side as we'd discuss expenses in a dream, then receive a check in the mail the very next morning. But as the story of Afghanistan began to unfold, its mystical aspects assumed center stage. Afghanistan was the most significant geopolitical event of the late twentieth century but it was clearly something more. Afghanistan had been a store-house of secret knowledge for many thousands of years. Kipling, the soldier's poet had written about its mystical allure and the U.S. Congress had even acknowledged the mystical powers of its people. In its report dated January 3, 1985 it requested the power of "the Mujihadeen leadership, through their mystical tribal communications network, put an end to the production of opium, morphine base and heroin in their territory." Isolated and withdrawn it had preserved ancient secrets in almost total obscurity, touched only by the occasional holy warrior, drug dealer and the most esoteric of the intelligence community.

But what did the intelligence community want with the esoteric secrets of mystical holy warriors? The dreams intensified. Faces from the distant past began to appear right in our living room. A BBC program on the ancient Celts presented the reconstructed face of a two thousand-year-old ritual sacrifice, thought to be a real "Grail" warrior called "Lindow Man." And as I faced my own image on the TV screen, my family responded with shock at the resemblance. Everything seemed to be connecting me to the past, linking me with some distant voice to fulfill an ancient purpose. That the purpose was linked to Afghanistan became clear when, while gathering historical data on the British Army's first attempt to conquer Afghanistan in the 1840's we came upon an old photograph.

The photograph was of an Irish-American mercenary who'd found his way to Afghanistan in the 1820's. He'd discovered the religion of Zoroaster settled in the mountains and married an Afghan Princess. He lived the real life of Kipling's fictional Man Who Would Be King and to my astonishment dressed himself in a plaid uniform with bell bottoms and a matching turban. It was the eight hundred year old man from our daughter's dream and Alissa confirmed it that day quite matter of factly. Afghanistan had been a profoundly difficult experience to weather, one that seemed to have had no purpose.

But thanks to Oliver Stone we had begun to find one and as we assembled Afghanistan the whole picture and my place in it began to emerge. Sometimes the images were frightening as I found myself projected into holographic settings that felt more than real. But as time passed and the voices grew clearer, I came to realize the entire process was bringing me home, and that home was the home of my Geraldine ancestors.

For me personally, I had found the path through Afghanistan and without knowing it, engaged a mythic quest. Afghanistan, the seat, the home of the most ancient civilization had opened a door into another dimension on the eve of the millennium and I had walked through. The work we had done for Oliver Stone ultimately revealed itself to be something far more than just a screenplay. It established a validity to a mythic dimension that we believe is becoming more and more important to us as our world reaches a vital crossroads.

There is nothing in the Voice that is either science fiction or fantasy. All of the technologies employed and their applications are already far from the drawing boards and affecting your lives in ways the waking public has yet to discover. Within a very short time, holography, biotechnology and telecommunications will change the idea of what we think we are, altering the very substance of matter itself. In fact Cyberspace has already changed the way we interact with the world and promises to draw us even deeper into other dimensions long before we even know where we're going.

In 1181 Geraldus Cambrensis, Gerald de Barry of Wales with_held his knowledge of those other "mythic dimensions" because he feared those in power would seek to control it. Now, eight-hundred years later it is time for the knowledge of those mythic dimensions to be revealed and shared. The power to know is available to all of us.

We now invite you to share that Voice and dream with us of the new worlds that we know will soon emerge to waking vision; worlds where all of our voices; past, present and future can be joined in unequaled harmony.

Paul Fitzgerald and Elizabeth Gould

THE KALENDS OF MAY 1170 A.D.

It all seemed so familiar, a kind of deja vu; the long wooden boat, the horses, the anticipation on the cold white faces of the men as the ships quietly slipped through the mist shrouded rocks at dawn and slid onto the beach. This was an invasion, there was no disputing that, a twelfth century Norman invasion.

The image was breathtaking as the boats roared onto the shore to the sound of screaming horses and shrieking steel. You could hear them as the knight's horses bolted into the surf and circled on the beach in a loud clanking swirl.

The barefoot young woman on the hill seemed fascinated by it too, almost drawn to it as the fierce iron men raised their banner; a blood red X and moved off the beach. The delicate, blond Siobhan had seen invaders before. Bands of wild, red-headed Vikings in their dragon ships had long plundered the coastal towns. But these men were different, she thought. They were quiet, almost solemn, as if war for them was somehow a sacred event.

That was when she spotted the young man in his black armor as he saddled his horse and prepared to move inland.

He fascinated her, the Black Knight with his pale skin and long chestnut hair. There was something about him that set him off from the others and as they headed up the narrow road she moved in through the yellow flowers for a better look.

Hidden by her long yellow hair, she lay quietly as they emerged from behind a rocky bend and passed. They were close, so close she could almost make out the words of their whispered prayers under the jangle of steel and the clop of hooves. It was a strange tongue, but she knew from her mother's daily attendance at the Christian chapel that the chanted words were Latin.

That was when she realized why these men were different. These were holy warriors, Christian holy warriors. But why were Christian holy warriors invading a Christian nation? And who was this Black Knight, whose prayers were now not among them. Had he sensed her eyes upon him and come up from behind?

She reached for a single yellow flower and picked it from its stem, then closing her eyes, she made a wish almost as if to draw him to her.

The Black Knight wheeled in surprise as the girl rose from the heather. Standing amidst the sea of yellow flowers, she appeared the image of nature itself and as she beckoned, it stopped him cold. He knew this woman, knew her from somewhere. But how was that possible?

***

The question was still on my mind as I struggled from the dream and found myself staring at the red letters of the digital clock in the half-light of the bedroom.

It was 5:55 on the morning of November 29 in the year of our Lord 2003, of that I was sure. The city was London, my name was Paul Fitzgerald and I had aged beyond my 52 years. I could feel the weariness in my bones as I rose from the bed and stared into the mirror. The dreams had been getting more real and more intense, and now they were taking a toll. In fact sometimes they didn't feel like dreams at all. They felt like memories—but whose memories I didn't know.

What was worse, the memories sometimes felt like they had followed me home, were pushing their reality into mine so forcefully I had begun to consider them as real. In very important ways this new reality had broken my narrow sense of the world, eliminated the conventional boundaries that I'd taken for granted all of my life and prepared me for something new. What that "new" something was, I was not yet prepared to accept. But as the waves of feeling washed over me, it felt as if the dream was somehow gathering all of its parts together and that somehow soon, it would emerge to absorb everything I considered real.

"Don't you love me the best?" I heard his voice whisper as I stared up into the dresser mirror. "The time has come for you to face the truth."

He was here, the darkened image of the Black Knight from my dream. I shook at the sight of him staring back at me from the other side of the mirror, his pale, white face framed in that cold black armor. For some reason his appearance was the nightmare I feared most, some lurking shadow drawing me into the past. Was it still a dream or was this reality? I sensed I had lost the ability to discern the difference. But as his cold, lifeless eyes faded from view I knew he had come to challenge me and if I didn't defeat him, he would draw me into his nightmare forever.

L

HYDE PARK, LONDON SUNDAY, NOVEMBER 29, 2003 A.D.

Hyde Park was crowded as my daughter Alissa and I trotted our horses out from their East Street stables for their much needed Sunday "stroll." Thanks to global warming, the growing hole in the ozone layer and an ominous shift in the Gulf Stream, British weather now resembled Miami's and despite the dire warnings of a few exasperated environmentalists, the whole city of London seemed to revel in it.

The horses loved it too, my white mare Juno, prancing and strutting her cadence just ahead of Alissa's black stallion, Attila, the way she had back in her traveling circus days. For fear they'd be packed off to a slaughter house, I'd picked the pair up after the last big top folded, but in a short time I found them to be a source of endless enjoyment.

At first I thought it strange how the horses had come to mean so much to me here in London. But then I seemed to enjoy many things here that had meant nothing to me back in the States.

It wasn't that I disliked the land of my birth. It was that America had never completely felt like home. Nothing in America seemed as genuine to me as the old world and its meanings and as my alienation grew I had fallen into the past.

That was why the image of the Black Knight lingered. Like a swimmer stirring the muck at the bottom of a dark pool, I'd raised something long dead and now he clung to me. As we trotted across the park, his silent presence seemed to hang over the conversation like a dark cloud.

"He was here again, wasn't he?" Alissa asked, spurring Attila on.

"He's always here now." I said to my daughter, a young woman whose intelligence and wit made her inquiries of my dream-life increasingly difficult to side step.

"Maybe you should see somebody about it then," she said, a look of concern growing in her eyes.

"I'm not crazy. I need to know who he is. I need to meet him on his own turf because I know he understands what I'm looking for."

Alissa huffed in genuine amazement. "On his own turf? How are you going to meet someone who lives in dream?" .

"I don't know yet. But when I do I will instruct him to dispose of Rick Kendall."

Alissa laughed deeply, the sadness in her eyes suddenly disappearing. "Then you'd better get started. Your lawyer called to say there's no way out of that contract. The publisher owned all the rights including sequels and Kendall's conglomerate bought the publisher. The book belongs to them."

I'd hoped against hope, but I suspected something like this was coming. Despite all my efforts to avoid it, Kendall had my story locked up and there was nothing I could do. The thought shot me back into the darkness—back into my experiences with the Black Knight. At night I was haunted by dark images of the past, stalked by my look-alike dressed in the black armor of a medieval assassin. By day, I was hemmed in on all sides by a book contract that had drawn me into the clutches of what was rapidly becoming an omniverse of huge "entertainment" conglomerates bent on controlling every means of human communication.

"He'll get nothing from me!" I said, spurring Juno toward a hedge row some hundred yards in the distance almost as if something inside me felt it could outrun the walls closing in around me.

Alissa knew where my rage sprang from and if she didn't support it, she at least accepted it as justified. For years, her mother and I had made our living by combing the world for controversial news stories and if we hadn't made a lot of money, we had conquered some difficult assignments.

It had been an exciting and dangerous profession. But we had survived—that was until we met up with Rick Kendall.

Kendall had gotten involved with our story on Afghanistan and from that moment on our lives had come crashing down. In my mind, I knew that Kendall wasn't entirely responsible, that each given our priorities, something was bound to go wrong. But it had been his callous, businesslike response to the accidental death of my wife that had prompted my anger and as time went on, I knew I'd never be able to forgive him.

"I know you blame him for what happened to Mom," Alissa yelled as she raced up beside me in an attempt to reason with me. "But that really wasn't his fault."

"He told us he'd back us Alissa. He told us to take the risks needed to get the story he wanted and no matter what he'd back us up. 'Don't worry. I'm the one they'll crucify,' he said. So we threw everything we had into it. This wasn't just another story, Alissa. This was going to break bigger than Watergate, bigger than Vietnam. And as soon as they turned up the heat up on him, he ditched and left us to the wolves. He's a coward and a liar, Alissa and he cost me my world."

"Then make him account for it!" Alissa shouted as Attila suddenly fell back.

I should have seen the look of alarm in Alissa's eye, but it wasn't until a second or two later that I saw the hedge looming ahead. I had no choice but to jump now and as I pulled hard on Juno's reins, the inertia drove us up and over until we landed on the other side.

It wasn't a difficult jump, not for Juno anyway. Jumping through hoops was her specialty. But my hoop jumping days were over. That was something I intended for Rick Kendall to know.

"You have to see him dad." Alissa said, as she trotted the black stallion around to me. "Mom would want it that way."

"I know, Alissa." I said as the idea sank in and I slowly regained a sense of control. "I'll give him a call in the morning."

FLEET STREET

The Newspaper headlines blared out the daily carnage as I cris-crossed the narrow, smoke-filled streets known to the world as the Mecca of tabloid journalism: IRA VOWS TO DESTROY "CITY"—IRISH BOMBS ROCK PALACE.

Outside of Hollywood, few places on earth catered to people's worst instincts better than the newspaper empires located on Fleet Street and none had been doing it for so long.

From the earliest days of England's Empire, Fleet had functioned as the unofficial voice of the realm, its newspapers cranking out the longed-for desires and official wis doms of the nearby Palace and the Bank of England while keeping the opposition in check with innuendo and hearsay. In return for this service, the crown had made the men who owned the presses "barons" of information.

Now, in many ways these barons were more powerful than the governments they operated under. And as the new millennium began, they were already extending their control into electronic realms not even dreamed of by Orwell.

Cellular phones, computers and the Internet tied the world together in an electronic web that only a decade before seemed like science-fiction. From outer-space, satellites could pinpoint a burglar crawling through a window or a Middle East dictator about to launch an attack, and the appropriate weapon stood ready to deal with either at a moments notice. Under the banner of better "marketing," the monitoring of humanity was now a twenty-four hour affair with every-thing from the number of toilet flushes, to your brand of toothpaste, available with the click of a mouse.

But even with all this, control seemed to be slipping away. Random acts of secular and religious violence were becoming an epidemic and as a last resort, security forces had been called out to patrol a city desperately trying to maintain calm.

Apparently, it was none to soon. London was a city under siege. Cobblestone streets that had once clamored with the cries of "Victoria reigns" and the brass bands of victorious armies now rang with the sound of ambulances and police cars, as camouflaged soldiers guarded strategic streets. Despite years of painstaking negotiations, a hardened core of Irish Republicans was out to break the perception the British government was still in control of anything. And after eight hundred years of armed struggle they seemed to be doing it.

In sixty years, the reality of an Empire that had once stretched over a third of the world's surface had shrunk to the province of Northern Ireland and the six square miles bordered by the gates of Buckingham Palace and the banks of the Thames.

Why the crown was so bent on holding onto its first and last colony seemed counter to the reality of the day, but without the Fleet street scandal-mongers holding the public's attention, there would soon be no reality at all.

"May I see your ID.," said the unkempt young man guarding the doors of Transitron, the latest and surely most powerful of the new multimedia conglomerates that were rapidly supplanting the power of nations.

"Will this do?" I said, pulling out a battered, old Massachusetts license from my wallet. "It's all I have with a picture on it."

"Paul Fitzgerald," he said, scratching a full days growth of beard. "Well. We'll see if it's you."

The guard wasn't pleased with this casual identification, of course. Security personnel liked everything neat, tidy and up-to-date in their bloodshot, angst-ridden universe of constant suspicion. But today it would have to do.

"You're lucky Massachusetts logged on to the international criminal data base back in '97," he said, feeding my driver's license into a nearby computer which scanned my image. "Terrorists can pass themselves off as almost anyone."

"Some people consider all Massachusetts' drivers to be terrorists," I replied, attempting to mask my sarcasm with a smile as the computer screen next to him blinked on and off like the latest 3-D video game. "What is that?" I asked.

The guard lifted his goggles from his eyes and turned to the screen.

"The ultimate in surveillance," he said proudly of the screen as it divided and subdivided into hundreds of separate locations within the building as if seen with a thousand sets of eyes. "With this, I have a positive ID on everyone that's entered this building all day and exactly what they're doing."

"So where do you hide the cameras?" I asked.

The guard smirked as he stamped my hand with a luminous green ink. "For your own protection, that must remain a secret. Welcome to Transitron."

I hated the security that constantly ate away at personal liberties and privacy. I hated police cars in my rear view mirror, searches at the ball park and body scans at the airport. But what I hated most was being told that stealing my freedom as a human being was all for my own protection. Modern life was a constant inquisition and nobody much minded. In fact few people seemed to care about the constant surveillance or the implications for what it meant. But I did. Sooner than later every human being on the face of the planet would be catalogued, profiled and labeled according to race, color and blood type, then stored in a huge computer memory according to DNA profile. Chips would be implanted to monitor the heart and liver function of the diseased or disabled and soon the public would cry for more. Sexual dysfunction and criminal behavior would be chipped out of existence and a brave new world of perpetually orgasmic, electronically regulated people would be born. The public's desire for more and better electronics would eventually replace the desire to grow and mature and I knew that one day soon, clever, thinking machines would outpace the people they were made to serve and the natural evolution of life as we knew it would end. I wondered how I would think when that day came. I wondered what I would do when I realized a silicon chip could think and feel every emotion I had ever had, emulate my every joy, experience my every thought. But as I watched my digitized face appear on a thousand tiny facets of the video wall behind the guard, all I could feel was rage. And the screen seemed to flicker in response almost as if it sensed my anger.

"Bloody hell!" The guard yelled as all the little squares disappeared indicating a power overload had whited-out the security system. "Not again."

He grimaced and moaned as his hands attacked the keyboard to his computer, vainly trying to bring the images back to life. But it was not to be. For some reason, at the same moment I'd seen my image, something had triggered the entire system to crash.

"You're cleared," he muttered as he manually extracted my license from the dead scanner. "But I'll be watching you."

I picked my license from the security desk and walked toward the elevators, past the huge company logo which spanned the lobby in six foot letters. After what I'd just witnessed, it seemed an ominous message:

A NEW MILLENNIUM AND TRANSITRON BRINGS IT TO YOU.

Transitron brings it *through you* was probably more to the point. "Transitron," the whole idea was in the name. Most scientists wouldn't admit to the esoteric side of their business, to the darker under workings, not to mention networkings that produced the so called electronic marvels of the twentieth century. On Wall Street it appeared all hard work, capital investment and research and development. And that was how it was sold to the public.

Few, if any, could recall that the origins of their "research" had emerged from ancient religious texts, secretly studied by social outcasts called heretics long before there had been anything formally considered as science at all.

In fact, the founder of Transitron himself, Lord Archibald De Clare had been an avid collector of such ancient obscurata. He'd actually come to believe that the long sought after goal of perfection through alchemical transformation desired by Renaissance men like John Dee, Sir Isaac Newton and Giordano Bruno could finally be achieved through the powers of the newly developing electronics.

It was an idea that would have gotten him burned at the stake in another era. But thanks to the military necessities of World War II, he'd been enthusiastically encouraged by state security and he had achieved a significant number of what were euphemistically called "breakthroughs" into the unknown.

Under the cover of the Cold War he'd continued these breakthroughs right up to the doors of human perception and so he'd named the company Transitron; "Through Electronics." The one question that remained thirty-three years after its founder's death was "through electronics to where?"

After my experience at the front desk I had the gnawing suspicion that my forced employment here would ultimately reveal that.

It was odd, I thought as I stepped from the glass walled elevator into the cold, glass corridors of Transitron. I would never have even thought to question the West's relentless drive for technology, had it not been for my own experiences in Afghanistan. Before then, history had just seemed a serious of random actions and reactions, unplanned or predicted. But after covering that war, I knew history, was a programmed event; planned, executed and reported by a privileged elite that had been at it for a long time.

Trying to find the meaning of Afghanistan and what had happened to me there had driven me from a linear Western view of reality and skewed my perception. And after a while I had come to see the world's events, its politics and wars, the course of history itself as an ancient and ongoing struggle between the forces of darkness and light with the ultimate goal being, the evolution of the human soul.

It was the course of this "evolution" that had been the subject of my first book, the Apostle's Diary, the book now controlled by Transitron. I found the idea of a legendary power broker like Lord Gilbert DeClare in control of my own personal avenue to the truth to be more than I could bear. I'd tried to comfort myself with the notion that it was only a business deal for him—just another cold-blooded raid on his way to building an empire.

But Lord De Clare was no simple-minded corporate raider, obsessed with the amassing of power to feed a maniacal ego. The rumors were, Lord De Clare was a "seeker" in a much greater game of hide and seek, and I didn't like the idea of him seeking me.

"Jerusalem was rocked today as suicide bombers struck the city causing hundreds of casualties. Callers representing the Holy Jihad movement claimed responsibility saying 'the day of judgement is at hand.'"

The screams of victims swirled from the overhead speakers like shrieking ghosts as I entered the sterile glass and steel office of the "thirty something" Rick Kendall.

He seemed older to me now. Not just in years either, but in manner. Gone was the brashness and the bravado. The job had turned him prematurely gray and the crisp lines of his expensive Italian suit only made him look wrinkled and tired.

As I walked to his desk I scanned the monitors that filled his office with economic chaos, starvation and general havoc. "Is this what you do?" I asked. "If I had to look at this all day I'd be under the desk, not at it."

"Somebody has to maintain the outposts of civilization," Rick answered, still distracted as he ran one hand through his hair while the other nervously punched the buttons of the black telephone on his desk.

"Benny. Did you see any missiles?" He said frantically as the voice at the other end of the phone struggled vainly to explain. "Then look closer. Look for the launchers, or the technicians, or the technicians' wives for god's sake. You've been to China. You know what they look like. They stick out."

Rick paused to listen, his eyes darting back and forth. "This is a visual medium Benny. I need pictures of missiles. I need images. I need to see what you're talking about. Now get me the pictures of those SCUD launchers or you can get yourself a job in radio."

"No pictures?" I asked, as Rick turned toward me, nervously pulling a pack of cigarettes from his pocket without offering one to me.

"Osama bin Laden sent his holy warriors over into Kashmir again so the Indians went to full alert. Pakistan responded by threatening a pre-emptive strike on India. One false move and South Asia goes up in smoke."

"Maybe you should censor it like you did Afghanistan." I added, deliberately taunting him with my memory of his own words. "After all. There's no point in getting people all excited about something that's totally beyond their control."

The response hit Rick in a sore spot.

"You still act like I caused Afghanistan all by myself, don't you?"

"I don't need to be reminded of what you caused in Afghanistan. If you had told people the truth about what we were doing in the first place maybe those Chinese missiles wouldn't be in Pakistan. Maybe Osama bin Laden would still be in Saudi Arabia selling insurance to oil sheiks and there wouldn't be a crisis. For ten years you knew we drew the Russians into Afghanistan and you lied about it. You and your friends had to turn the whole affair into a holy war. So this is what you get."

"I knew this wouldn't be easy, Paul. But we're going to have to put away our differences."

"And give me a reason I should want to do that?"

Kendall turned cold. "Because Lord Gilbert wants your book. And what Lord Gilbert wants, Lord Gilbert gets."

Rick had thrown me a left hook and I felt like I'd been punched. Our last encounter had been over the issue of Afghan "blowback," the fallout from America's secret war there and it had been bitter. But now it was getting ugly.

Following our last meeting, American trained Mujihadeen holy warriors had gone on to blow up the World Trade Towers, bomb a half dozen U.S. embassies and trigger a nuclear alert by invading the Indian province of Kashmir. Their stated ambition had been to kill 250,000 people alone at the Trade Towers, but their ambitions were global. Afghanistan had become the home to Osama bin Laden, a man whose ultimate goal was nothing less than the destruction of the Western World and the establishment of God's Kingdom on earth. How he planned to accomplish this was still a mystery, but it was known he was welcomed as a savior by much of the Moslem world and was probably getting military support from the Chinese.

The unraveling of the Soviet Union in Afghanistan had unleashed vast stockpiles of nuclear weapons onto the world's arms markets, and now with its southern border essentially unguarded, those stockpiles were flowing through Afghanistan into every country of the Middle East.

But what seemed the capstone to this incredible story was that the terror had not begun under the influence of the "Evil Empire," or at the urging of some Islamic terrorist like Kaddafy or Saddam, but by America itself—and Rick and dozens of men like him had kept the lid tightly shut on the secret so American democracy would not interfere.

Rick knew I'd warned him about the dangers of this lie but he hadn't listened. "Spiking" my story on Afghanistan had been a "career decision." Buying my book guaranteed his career would continue— maybe. There was something different about him this time. The ever present confidence, not to mention the arrogance was gone and replaced by nervousness. I couldn't help wonder if the consequences of his lying were beginning to pile up.

"Just give me a chance to show you what we're doing here. Then you can tell me whether you want to go on hating the world or not." He said, stepping out from behind his desk, while directing me to following him down the corridor. "You have to work with us Paul, so you might as well know who we are."

"Transitron started out as a manufacturer of electronic components for the defense establishment and pioneered the application of light-bearing technology for data transmission," he said. "Few people understood the quantum aspects of light transmission when we first got started, so we now pretty much control the field. Laser discs, CD ROM, fiber optics were all the brainstorm of our founder, Lord Archibald De Clare and under his son Gilbert we've moved to corner the market on telecommunication world-wide."

I followed Rick down the glass corridor as he pointed to the various departments.

"From these offices we transfer ninety-two percent of all international telephone calls and through subsidiaries, operate two thirds of the world's satellite traffic. By this time next year, we'll own it all. We run five hundred channels and thirty-two web sites twenty-four hours a day. Thanks to our founder, we control all the basic patents on virtual reality and our investments in biotechnology ensure we'll be on the ground floor with biologically enhanced electronics."

The idea stopped me cold. "Biologically enhanced products?"

Rick waved a hand dismissively. "Come with me, I'll introduce you to Perry."

Rick had me follow him down the hall and into the elevator, then down the glass tube to one of the numerous levels of sub-basement. Below were a labyrinth of glass walled corridors beyond which could be seen huge banks of computers blinking in the darkness. The entire scene gave the impression of one huge machine and after walking for what seemed five minutes we came to a set of steel doors. Inside, a young man sat motionless, staring vacantly at a bank of monitors as his hands grasped a small black machine with shiny gold letters that read Dream Catcher.

"Perry is our guinea pig. Right now he's battling Kirk Douglas in Sparticus," Rick said, his voice echoing off the empty walls. "Next he'll have a drink at Rick's cafe with Humphrey Bogart and Claude Rains, have a dance with Julia Roberts and maybe even go to bed with Marilyn Monroe."

I glanced at the monitors as Rick removed the Dream Catcher from Perry's lap and withdrew what seemed like a small glass marble. Then, replacing the marble with one drawn from his pocket I watched as the image of a sneering Douglas, was replaced with Bogart.

Rick marveled at the image of the young intern from Sussex as he postured in front of Claude Rains. "Imagine the possibilities of this. Look at him. He's entirely lost in it. Just like a dream."

I had to admit I was amazed. It was like watching a dream, only it wasn't a dream, it was an old movie but with a whole new cast of characters. "What is it?" I asked. "How do you do this?"

"Coded Holograms. But here's the best part," Rick said, as he flipped a switch on a nearby console—and the dream, that just a second before was confined to the TV sets, suddenly engulfed us. "Imagine the world you want, the life you never had," Rick shouted over the din of Rick's cafe, "and you can have it."

The impact was shocking. The image—3 dimensional. Then I reached out to touch Bogart. "Jesus, he's real." Bogart turned and laughed. "Louis, pour this guy a drink. Maybe it'll calm him down."

I yelled to Rick. "I thought you needed some kind of body hardware, a machine for virtual reality."

"You do. But this isn't virtual reality. It's the next step beyond virtual reality. For all intents and purposes, it's real, reality."

"But how?"

"That stamp on your hand." Rick said, reaching for a blister pack on the shelf and extracting a tiny capsule the size of an aspirin. "Dissolvable micro-chips so small they can interact with a human brain cell. One capsule, one swipe on your wrist with that stamp and your brain opens up to them, becomes a receiver for 48 hours."

I raised my hand to examine the luminous green stamp and my head swirled. "You son of a bitch."

"Sorry about the disorientation. But it wears off.." Rick pulled up a chair and sat down. "It's the quantum part of the physics. Think of it all as light, waves and particles. Sometimes light is a wave, like an idea with no substance. Sometimes it's a particle. Think of something long enough and the particles build up into the form of the idea. Quantum physics tells us the observer can make a dream real and everybody knows how real a dream is when you're in it. Heart rate, metabolism, the whole brain is reacting the same as it would to wakefulness. The only difference is the brain wave that governs the dream knows its only a wave and not a particle and shuts the body down, so you won't hurt yourself."

"So you alter the wave?"

For the first time Rick smiled. "And the dream automatically projects itself outside your head. Nobody else can see it. But to you it's just as real as reality itself. All those tales about gods and goddesses, mythical monsters and giants? Well, we found out how it works."

So absorbed in the dream, Perry barely even noticed as Rick took the small black box from his hands and flipped the off-switch causing an effect that was nearly as startling as the dream itself.

In an instant the room seemed to collapse in on itself, folding along crystalline lines like a triangle, from three dimensions to two and then to one until we were again surrounded by cold steel walls and the banks of blinking computers beyond.

"Without the signal, its only a dream in your head. With the signal it's reality," Rick said as an annoyed Perry shook himself awake.

The idea was sinking in. Neuro-chemists, physicists, psychologists and philosophers had been bouncing around new ideas on reality for most of the decade and the jury was still out as to exactly what "it" was. In fact, the more the masters of the physical world, the physicists studied it, the less substantial any reality seemed. Now, with the new capabilities of electronics, the human race was on the verge of escaping its own sense of material being and men like Gilbert De Clare were wiring the world, waiting like new gods to escort us on our trip.

"But how did it get out of my head?"

Rick nervously ran his hand through his hair. "That's the part we didn't plan for. It just happened. We think its some latent capacity in the brain for projecting what we think is reality. We call it the restructuration effect."

"The what?"

Rick seemed concerned. "Re-ordering the paradigms of thought we use to construct reality. Like a painting. Picasso's images don't look the same as Van Gogh's. Picasso is more primal, more universal. But both images are constructs of the artists reality of the world."

"We don't live in a Van Gogh or a Picasso."

"Appearance wise, no. But in terms of the mathematical construct of our understanding we do. What we choose to listen to, choose to wear, read, hear, . . . think can all be broken down mathematically. Project that number along a time-place coordinate at the speed of light and you can construct any world you want, purely in thought."

"Like a hologram."

Rick smiled. "After your Afghanistan adventures this shouldn't seem a surprise. Afghanistan was one of the first places on earth that myth transformed from thought into conscious reality—the home of the god Mithra. Think about the etymology of the word. Myth and Ra. Truth and Light. It's a thought form brought to life. That's why we consider it the place where the Western Dream was born. Isn't that what you said in the Apostle's Diary?

He'd caught me off guard. "Yes. But we're in the material world Rick. There are still rules."

Rick averted his eyes. "We're surpassing the physical limitations every day. I know, I've seen it. Back in the 30's a German philosopher began looking at the origins of human consciousness. He determined that the narrow, rational, three dimensional way we viewed the world wasn't only holding us back from understanding new discoveries in physics, it was holding us back from where our consciousness wanted to take us. He broke the development of human consciousness down into stages, the magical, the mythical and the rational. In the magical, our understanding was childlike and so was our behavior. In the mythical, the gods and goddesses were real and could be appealed to for help. Then in the rational we narrowed the world to only those things we perceived could be controlled and created the world we live in today. The problem is, the material world has reached its limits too. We've reached a dead end. Until now. "

"And now we're ready for the fourth plane of reality, the culmination and synthesis of all preceding experience." I said, realizing how seriously Rick had taken my first book. "But nobody can predict what it will look like or when it might happen. If it does happen."

"It will happen. And with our technology we're prepared for it."

I must have looked confused. "What I was talking about was a spiritual awakening. Not a new use for electronics."

"It's what's in store for us. The synthesis of everything we've been— projected outside our heads and given life. You know, the awaited fourth dimension. Look, I'm not a scientist, I'm a news manager, but there are people who can materialize the wounds of Jesus Christ, right down to the nails in their hands and everybody can see them without our chips. It's called stigmata and it's been going on now for at least 2000 years. People have been reporting UFOs for two millennia, others see the Blessed Virgin. At least with a little help from our chips everybody can control what they see."

"And you can send that signal from here?" I asked, needing to confirm my suspicions.

Rick nodded, hoping that such powers would impress me beyond question.

"Then you're absolutely insane." I responded.

Rick slumped. "What are you talking about?"

"Look at the news. It's chaos already and you want to go and turn everything into make-believe?"

"It's just the beginning. When we get started . . . " Rick said, his voice turning ever more serious. "You saw the monitors back there in my office. It gets worse every day. People hate each other and they're tearing the world apart. At least this way they can think they have a life."

I motioned toward Perry who'd resumed his personal immersion into dreamland with Marilyn Monroe. "You call that a life?"

As I stared at Perry the multiple screens that dotted the building again flashed to white, blinking on and off like a bank of bloodshot eyeballs. "Are you going to tell me what that is?"

Rick mumbled in an unconvincing effort to hide his concern. "The process is too new to be sure exactly. Quite honestly Paul, we didn't expect to get so far, so fast. Interference is getting in from somewhere. We thought at first it might be someone trying to shut us down. But now we know it's not that."

"So what is it?

Rick bit his lip. His nerves strained. "Some kind of quantum aberration. A dimensional crossover? Maybe something even mystical. You talked a lot about stuff like that happening to you in Afghanistan."

"So that's why your Lord Gilbert wants my book."

"You did talk about the way the Holy Warriors could dream their way into the Russians' camp. I think the Senate Select Committee called it the mystical communications network?"

"And now somebody's dreaming their way into your circuitry." I offered.

"We don't know that for sure."

"Did you really believe you could activate Afghan holy warriors on the eve of the Apocalypse and keep it quiet? Holy war isn't some freak show to put on your Web site and advertise with Coca Cola. These men are empowered. They close their eyes and do what your blinking machines do and you can't make up for that with electronics. Their power is mystical and it's real, just the way it was for the Crusaders in 1099."

"And so is Lord Gilbert's request. You have a new manuscript that describes these things in detail. Lord Gilbert owns an option on it. The sooner you show it to him the sooner this entire matter will be resolved."

The phone rang. As Rick lifted the cell phone from his pocket I lifted a Dream Catcher aggie to the light and traced the intricate electronic patterns that wove reality into form. It was incredible how such a small thing could produce such results—perhaps even magical.

Rick barely noticed as I pocketed it for good luck, pausing intently as he received instructions. "Yes, Lord Gilbert. No, Lord Gilbert. I'll tell him." He rang off as if he'd been cut off abruptly then paused. His look was glassy and distant, nearly the opposite of what it had been a moment ago. "Most people would be envious to have a contract and an eager publisher waiting for their manuscript." He said averting his eyes. "But since I know you're not like most people, all I can say is I'll give you 48 hours to hand it over. If I haven't heard from you by then, you'll be hearing from me."

The screens seemed to flicker even brighter this time, but I said nothing as I turned my back on Rick Kendall and found my way out. There was nothing left to say. I was fighting with a feudal baron named Lord Gilbert De Clare who had won this battle and probably the war.

I had 48 hours to conjure up a solution. But as I faced the cold December winds outside the Transitron building, I could think of nothing but the darkness about to descend and the ghostly faces of those who had walked these streets before me.

JUICY JOHN PINK

I felt totally alone, perhaps even more solitary than I'd ever felt as I walked the cold, damp streets of London, past the Black friars Bridge and into the antique Underground station nearby. For me, the dream realm had become a separate reality, a new dimension, more real than the one I awoke to every morning. Despite the occasional appearance of the Black Knight it had become a place where I could find answers. But after seeing what Lord Gilbert's Dream Catcher chip could do to reality I was more confused than ever what my dreams really were. Perhaps, the increasing body of thought about dreams was true. Dreams weren't a product of our sleeping minds. We were a product of our dreams and as the Big Dream came to an end we had to wake up to a new reality. With the exception of Alissa I had little left to care for anyway. If this was the new dream, I didn't like it—and as I sank deeper into the Underground station, it seemed as if I was walking into the depths of sleep forever. Even the busy station wasn't enough to shake me from the feeling and as I walked to the platform staring into the future I realized there was none.

I recalled that the only other times I'd ever felt like this, something had always happened to change my life. It had been magical really. Meeting my wife Elizabeth had been like that and so had Afghanistan, but looking around at the crowded platform it appeared an unlikely setting for magic. There was the smell of wet wool, the mumbling of passengers and the noise of the approaching train and that was it.

It wasn't until I felt a nudge about waist high, that I noticed the little man, a midget, in some distress. In his super-human effort to reach the train he had wormed his way to the very edge of the platform and now he stood, feet dangling over the pit, his large oval face growing tense with fear.

It was at that moment that the crowd suddenly surged, pushing hard on the little man and in an instant I found myself reaching for him. He nearly took me with him as I grabbed his shirt collar and dug in, his body swaying and eyes bulging as the old train barreled into the station with a roar and a hiss of brakes. But in that split second before the plunge I'd managed to stop his descent and in another second I'd righted the little man so that by the time the train screeched to a stop, he had miraculously adjusted himself to his dilemma.

"Mind the gap," the midget announced proudly as the doors slid open and he hopped onto the train as if nothing extraordinary at all had happened.

"Yes. Quite," I gasped as I stepped over the divide and made my way to the end of the car, unable to take my eyes off the strange little man now sitting opposite me as the train groaned off, down the tracks.

"Oldest section of track in the oldest part of town." The little man said, smiling back at me as he wobbled back and forth while chewing on a large wad of what I assumed was tobacco. "Not the most reliable."

"Or safe, either." I added, thinking back to the incident on the platform.

"It all works out," the midget continued, his grin now resembling a crescent moon. "John Pink's the name," he said as he seemed to screw himself more comfortably into his seat. "My friends call me Juicy."

"Paul," I replied, now feeling somewhat self-conscious.

"American?" Juicy asked.

"Once," I answered, as I tried to keep memories from flooding back.

"Oh! Bit-o'sarcasm there. Never going back?" Juicy John pressed, his curiosity and rapid-fire style, unhindered by my lack of engagement. "I like it here, too; the history, the blitz, the Queen, Windsor Castle and the Tower. For me it's like it all hap pened yesterday. Did you know they spiked the heads of the King's enemies on London bridge?"

"Yes, I'd heard." I said, trying not to seem annoyed.

"And do you know why?" The little man said in a whisper as if sharing a deep and dark secret, his little legs swinging back and forth excitedly. "Because there was magic in them. Big magic." He said moving his hands in a broad arc. "The strongest got buried outside the walls. And they're down there still, watching . . . waiting—guarding against what might come. Some say if you listen hard enough on a dark night you can hear them talking and if you're lucky they'll talk to you."

The train suddenly jerked as the main lights flickered and the motor died, slowing the rickety beast to a stop not far down the darkened tunnel from where we had started. Except for Juicy—who let out an immediate string of curses—there was little panic. Ever since World War II, Londoners had grown used to this kind of inconvenience. But the events were growing more frequent now and people were beginning to wonder.

"Ladies and gentlemen," the crackling voice of the intercom announced as the emergency lights flicked on. "A security emergency has caused a temporary power outage in this part of London. Please remain seated until power is restored."

People sighed as the term, "IRA" was muttered and faces stared accusingly at each other. But to me the delay didn't matter. In fact, as the lights went out, I'd almost hoped the ground would swallow me up. But Juicy John Pink wasn't happy. As long as he had my ear, I was going to share in his discomfort.

"I'm getting out," Pink said as he squirmed around in his seat, trying to see outside into the darkness of the tunnel. "And so should you."

"Out where?" I asked, as I pondered what new and strange fate had caused this little man to cross my path.

"There!" The midget said, pointing to the tunnel with one hand while he grabbed at the collar of his shirt, the one I'd yanked out of place by saving him. "Last time this took six hours and I can't breathe now. It's the smell of all that wet wool, ya'know?"

"O.K. But how do we do it?" I asked, trying to humor the man.

"Follow me." He said as his little legs climbed down from the bench and into the aisle.

With amazing agility the little man squeezed under the passengers with squeals and shouts, quickly opening a path through the crowd. Then, his head bobbing to the surface as he reached the open emergency door, he waved madly for me to follow.

"C'mon!"

For the moment I was relieved by the midget's departure. I hadn't counted on a companion and if I had it surely wouldn't have been a four foot man with bad manners and a worse sense of balance. But Juicy John Pink was not going to leave me alone and as I sat back and took a deep breath, I heard the sound of tapping on the window behind my head.

"Quick, or you'll miss your chance." He beckoned, face pressed against the glass.

I couldn't help grimace as the other passengers stared. It was against my instincts to leave the car, let alone leave it with a strange little man. Juicy John was obviously deranged, leaving a subway car in the middle of a dark tunnel, especially after he'd just come so close to being killed. But there was something in those dark little eyes that said, you'd better listen to me, and after a moment of not-so-profound meditation I politely moved through the passengers and in an instant, found myself on the train's boiler plated platform.

"Now what do we do?" I asked as I stood on the platform staring into the darkness, looking for the short little man with the oval face.

"Quick as a spark. Jump into the dark!" The voice said from somewhere beyond the train.

It had been instinct—pulling the little man back from the oncoming train. Now it was instinct again—jumping into the empty pit.

"Where are you?" I yelled as I groped around in the dark gritty tunnel, barely able to discern the outline of the rails against the distant signal lights.

"Quick. This way!" The voice called as I suddenly felt myself being pulled to my feet and tugged up the tracks. "We've got to go before they find us."

"Isn't that the point?" I asked, as I turned and saw the flicker of flashlights from down the tunnel.

"That is decidedly not the point," Juicy John said as he forcefully pulled me in the opposite direction away from the train and up the tracks.

"But the light?" I demanded.

"Don't follow the light," Juicy John said in a tone that struck fear into me. "Not this time. Come."

I thought I was mad, stumbling along into the darkness away from a rescue team, a strange little midget my only companion—until all at once, I felt the thump of an explosion under my feet.

I didn't have to wait for Juicy John this time. In an instant the force of a tremendous explosion filled the tunnel with a blinding white light and I was blown down, face first into the pit.

A moment later the debris from the train roared over us and when I lifted my head, all that remained were six sets of wheels and a flaming wreck.

"You knew," I said as I stared at the midget, busily brushing himself off as he struggled to his feet.

"I guessed," he said gravely.

"But why did you choose me to save?" I asked, trying to settle myself down as I watched the flames dance over the little man's face.

"You saved me," he said, simply and to the point. "And that has put me in your debt."

I stood for a moment and stared at the wreckage and marveled. Standing on the platform of the station only minutes before, I had seen my life at an end with no meaning and no future.

Now I was standing in a subway tunnel covered in soot, with a prophetic midget named Juicy.

Life was strange and getting stranger but I was in no position to refuse now. Smoke was filling the tunnel. If there was to be a future I knew it had to start now. I turned to the little man and patted him on the head. Then without a word, we began our escape.

TRANSITRON

The view from the penthouse suite at the Transitron building was limited to a few square miles bordering the Thames in the usually foggy London sky but within those few hundred acres, a thousand years of history had been forged and a world had been ruled. This was of little consequence to Rick as he reported upstairs for duty, but to Lord Gilbert, Transitron's chief executive officer it was as primary as a corporate balance sheet. Tiny London's architecture, its hundreds of churches and Cathedrals packed into a square mile area was sacred architecture built on hallowed ground and he wanted Rick to know it.

"You see that building," Gilbert said, his face to the sun in such a way that Rick saw no more of him than a shock of red hair hidden in shadow. "That is the Templar Church, dedicated by the Patriarch of Jerusalem himself, in the year 1185. Under its vaulted dome lie the original Crusaders. Men whose dream of a golden future for mankind sanctified England's destiny."

"I see," said Rick, unimpressed with the historical lecture.

"No, you don't." Gilbert said, annoyed with Rick's casual interest. "Had it not been for the Templar's exploration of Jerusalem and the East, none of what you see around you would be here today. Law, banking, finance, the very basis of trade itself can all be laid to their discipline, their sacrifice and their sacred rule. They made this world a reality my dear Richard. Nothing less than reality."

"I hadn't realized," Rick said politely.

"Then you must begin to," Gilbert said quietly drawing back. "Because it is that reality that we spread around the world from here—that culture that we define as us, the culture that enables us to run the world. It is our paradigm, our hologram. And if you cannot understand how it is constructed. You will never be able to sustain it beyond the present."

"I'm sorry Lord Gilbert, history was never my strong suit. I'm more of a hardware guy," Rick said, biting his lip.

"There's a place for hardware." Gilbert said chuckling to himself. "In fact where would we be without it. But as guardians of the future, we must remember what we are here to do with that hardware." Gilbert pointed across the river to the huge five-hundred foot Millennium Ferris wheel opposite the Houses of Parliament. "That's why we built that Millennium Wheel on the opposite side of the Thames: "To remind us of the first thousand years of that future and open the door on the next."

"Which is why I'd like to get on with the day's business," Rick said impatiently. "There's a full agenda."

"Of course." Gilbert said, his tone dripping with sarcasm. "I thought perhaps if you saw it from my perspective you could better assume the duties your job description requires."

"Which duties are you referring to?" Rick asked, chastened but curious.

"The book, man. I could see by your threats that you mean to do business. Does he?"

"He's a difficult man, Lord Gilbert," Rick said, showing the frustration of his meeting with Paul. "Whatever he knows, he's not about to let go of it."

"And that is what makes it valuable." Gilbert replied, raising a finger to accent the point. "If he is the inheritor, then he must guard the knowledge like the Grail itself, which means in the end he will lead us exactly to what we're looking for."

"And what are we looking for?" Rick asked.

Lord Gilbert paused, his eyes lost deep in introspection. "The truth Mr. Kendall. The light and the truth!"

Rick strained to remain calm. "Then do you want me to have him followed?"

Gilbert laughed as he walked to his ornately carved antique desk and sat down in his huge leather chair.

"Dearest Richard, when you've been in business as long as me, you realize some things are simply not necessary."

Rick stood for a moment as if waiting for Gilbert to say more, to instruct, to let him in on what was so important about the book, but he remained silent. Only when Rick was out the door and safely beyond earshot did he mumble something. But it didn't sound very business-like.

Neither was what Gilbert did next, as he reached beneath his desk for a large antique box. Cradling it in his arms like a pet cat, he traced the ancient Celtic swirls of the snake-like embroidery to its jewel encrusted eyes, then caressed the lid of the box with his long bony hands.

"We need for Paul to remember," he said as he opened the box, revealing a stream of white light that seemed to fill the room. "We need for Paul to remember everything."

Gilbert was surrounded by the light now, causing the TV screen and lights on the ceiling to blink violently as if blasted by some spasm of energy. Then, burning white hot for an instant they burst, leaving Gilbert alone in the darkness, illuminated only by the intense white light of the box.

He remained that way for a long moment, as if absorbing some powerful drug until he began to shake. Then with a weak cry that seemed to say he could take no more, he closed the lid.

GHOSTS

The train hadn't taken us very far from where we'd started, leaving us under the oldest section of London. But the dark Underground was a haunted cavern filled with waterlogged, derelict tunnels that snaked off in every direction and I soon feared we were lost.

The subway was old, the oldest in the world actually and branched out into a half dozen directions, some now derelict, others just appearing that way. Two world wars had broken the Empire's finances and though Maggie Thatcher had dazzled the world with her "supply side economics," the supply remained safely beyond the reach of the city's oldest form of transportation.

The original nineteenth century excavations had cut through the heart of the old city and now the old tunnels were as much a relic to the faded glory of Empire as the old Roman ruins they periodically exposed.

In fact the whole place reeked of the misty past. Not the kind the textbooks or Hollywood gave us, but the real subterranean past that our very history was built on. Here underground were the bones of western society, preserved alongside the buried plague victims and the unpleasant memories of a thousand years of conquest. Down here with the unexploded German bombs and the headless corpses were the rotted pilings of Western Civilization with its Norman Forts and Elizabethan dungeons, rusted girders and broken dreams. Here in the dark all things were equal, life and death, dream and reality. Here in the dark, time stood still.

You could still hear the screams as the rack snapped shut, the bones cracked, the sinews tore and souls departed. Maybe this was where we'd lost our dreams; in the stinking dungeons. Maybe it was here we were taught not to dream under pain of death or worse, the pain of crushed hope. Maybe that was why we embraced the technology, the drugs and that elusive thing called progress, for fear the wheel of life might return us to this.

Americans didn't know much about these places and the feelings they evoked. We had no Bastille, no Tower of London, no tradition of oppression and conquest, of torture buried under our cities. We'd had no incendiary bombs dropped on us from above by angry Nazis, never been subjugated to another ideology or race. But most of the world had and the memories remained, waiting for just the right soul to stumble on them in the dark.

We knew so really little about how we got here, how fanatical our ancestors could be about their truth, about their reality. No wonder as we staggered into the new millennium, it was so hard to know where we were going.

"Where is the exit?" I asked, growing tired of the damp and the darkness.

Juicy John only remained reassuring. "Just up ahead, around the bend. Can't you feel it?" Juicy asked, seeming surprised.

I looked around at the pools of water and lifted a soaking foot to show my discomfort. "This is what I feel."

"You have to listen. Open up to the voices," Juicy said with a smile.

I listened and for a moment I thought I did actually hear something coming from the tunnel up ahead, something low and rhythmic rising off the tunnel floor and echoing off the damp moss covered walls. I tried to ignore it. But Juicy was filling my imagination with images and as we followed along the dark tunnel I could almost see the buried souls of England's past emerging in front of me.

"Hear the rack snap shut and the heads roll—the Nazi bombs and the bell toll? Who was their target, my dear old yank? Was it Windsor Castle or Rothschild bank?" As Juicy's smile grew larger than a

Cheshire cat I thought about the little town of London up above us and how desperate the Germans had been to destroy it.

"The City," as it was known was actually a tiny place, the self-contained financial heart of Britain no more than a medieval village in actual size. For all the hugeness that its Empire once represented, it still had the feel of the small, intimate town of London with its old ways.

Admittedly, some of those "ways" were a little strange. One of them—an ancient ritual still carried out every morning at 10:30—saw five "wise men" sit in the opulent Gold room of the Rothschild Bank to divine the world price of bullion. It was a ceremony that ensured the healthy circulation of the "blood" of international commerce but I couldn't help wonder if in some back room, hidden from view an ox wasn't occasionally gored to ensure the ceremony's efficacy.

Next door, Baring's Bank had financed England's armies against Napoleon's and with victory got the Middle East's resources in return. It was a fundamental aspect of warfare most citizens never considered, but it was money, not tactics or ideology that usually decided the outcome of geopolitical struggles.

Right next to "The City" sat Westminster where the Royals had governed since 1066. Much was said about their figurehead status as titular rulers of the realm, but the Queen's power was still very real. Of all the heads of state that had fallen to the age of rationalism, from Marie Antoinette to Tzar Nicholas, this "irrational" rule of blood was not to be denied the next millennium.

The Royals were as heavily invested in the future as they were in the past, but with their creaking, groaning style it was hard to see what they had to offer.

Yet still, even Hitler had wanted the Royal family kept alive to rule within their Third Reich once they had conquered. As I set my ear to the darkness, I wondered if perhaps there wasn't something the Nazis understood about the past that we had long since forgotten.

"Can you hear them?" Juicy said as he slogged, knee high through the dim light. "Ancient Druids sacrificing their kings to the mother of nature? Romans praying in her buried temples for the birth of their sun god? The union of heaven and earth, right here on the banks of the Thames, the Hieros Gamos, the sacred marriage."

"The Hieros Gamos," I thought. What did Juicy John know of the primeval marriage ceremony that inaugurated the earthly King as the medium between the sun god and the female spirit of the earth?

"The secret is more than meets the eye. It's why you're here, to find out why." He said, pointing toward a light down the tunnel.

I ran towards it as fast as I could. It was a secret all right—an archway—illuminated by an old iron work-light mounted on the wall nearby. "It's here." I shouted at my companion, as I turned to thank him. "It's the door." But the midget was nowhere in sight. All I could hear of the strange little man was a faint laugh from down the tunnel and a whispered echo, repeating his last message: "The secret is more than meets the eye. It's why you're here, to find out why."

I stopped for a moment and stared into the darkness. Juicy John Pink had led me to the exit, but now I was alone. I turned toward the archway. It was ancient, probably medieval; some secret passage down to the river used by the Black Friars to sneak past the king's tax agents.

A chill ran up my spine as I lifted the work-light from its ring and poked it inside. The chant I'd heard earlier seemed to grow louder and as I stepped inside the arch and climbed the old stone staircase I realized the strange little man must have deposited me at the door to a church.

There were probably hundreds of such doors to the hundred or so churches all over and under the City of London. England's politics, particularly its religious polit ics, had seen some of the worst sectarian violence in history and there were probably numerous instances when a quick escape had been necessary. Surely, places like this would still be well maintained and probably bustled with hundreds of curious tourists from sunup to sundown searching for the lost voices of the past.

I was sure of it now. But as I reached the crest of the stairs the chanting stopped. And as I twisted the iron ring on the old wooden door I suddenly found myself in the midst of a ceremony that was by no means intended for tourists. Suddenly I found myself in what seemed a smokey dream, standing in the middle of some great twelfth century church, torches blazing from their iron torchiers halfway up the steep stone walls.

I couldn't see the service or even the alter. All I could see was them, the Black Knights—an army of them dressed in black from head to toe, boot heels clicking on the gray stone floor, their dull black helmets shielding their faces; filing out of the pews and into the aisle.

Then one of them pulled off his head gear and said; "What do you think? Are you ready to join us?"

The man's face was so gentle, so full of color against the stark black and white background it took me by surprise. "I suppose I was trained for this somehow, the Sisters that taught me were always looking for a few good men," I said, caught off guard by the question. "But I never saw myself doing it."

Then, as we neared the back of the church, I saw a group of nuns sitting on the stone floor quietly examining a large pile of books, almost as if my comment had called them forth.

"Those are my nuns," I said to the Black Knight as I watched each select a book, briefly scan the pages, then discard it. "Sisters of Providence. The ones who taught me as a boy. What are they doing here?"

The Black Knight smiled when I said that, a comely smile. And then he said. "They're here to remind you of your obligation to your lord and master. It's not too late to change your mind."

I don't know what possessed me to say it, but at that moment I looked toward the top of the Cathedral and shouted in a loud voice. "I renounce you." But my escape was blocked by the other Knights and in the next moment the Black Knight placed his hand on my shoulder.

"Come with me," he said. As I turned to face him my head began to swim and in an instant I found myself riding on a storm. Soon I was spiraling into a vortex, riding into the darkness with the Black Knight at my side. "Hold on," he said in a voice that resembled the sound of crushed glass.

And so I held, and what passed before me seemed all too familiar. The dream was alive and I was in it. And in a moment I knew I was very far away.

JERUSALEM

My head spun and my body ached as I awoke, my head resting against a stone wall. I was somewhere beyond the church of the Black Knight, but where I didn't know. But when I rubbed my eyes and looked around a familiar feeling came over me, old but exact and I knew immediately where it was.

This was Jerusalem 1099 A.D., in a spot I had long ago visited. I tried to remember back. Why had the Black Knight brought me here? There was something buried inside the city—something I needed to get home. But what was it?

The heavy weight of the chain mail, the smokey smell of the camp-fires and the look, that special look of the holy city soon brought back the memories. It was the stone—the mythical stone from a long-ago palace of light, hidden somewhere within the city walls. No one in my lifetime had ever seen it. No one was sure it really ever existed.

But it felt good to remember, to know again in simple terms what one's life was about. There was no subtlety to life here—no possessions of note, except what mattered—steel helmet, thick brown leather belt and the sharpest of swords with which to impress your inquiries. I was a Crusader with a purpose and as I saw the camp-women who'd broken through the lines to fill their brown clay jugs at the Watergate, the memory of the whole experience flooded back.

Even in non-Muslim households in Jerusalem it was easier for a woman to wear the veil, knowing they would be treated with respect.

But the rag-tag army of vagabonds that followed the Crusaders observed no such custom—instead they taunted these defenseless women. I could sense the panic growing as the men surrounded them, singling one of them out as the easiest prey—lifting her skirt and snapping at her like a pack of wolves. I found myself to be disgusted with their behavior, their wantonness and cowardliness in the shadow of the holy city. I could feel the righteousness of God flowing within me, and as I fell on them they felt God's wrath.

The veiled woman seemed to barely notice as she scrambled to pick up the broken pieces of terra cotta urn that had fallen from her shoulders during the scuffle. Only for one brief instant when I caught her eye did she acknowledge, and then she was gone.

I surveyed the city. It looked impregnable. Despite our numbers, scaling the walls would be impossible. A siege could take months and the army was already underfed and sickly. We needed a miracle to gain entry, a miracle or a magic spell. And at that moment I somehow knew how that spell could be had.

STRONGBOW THE FIRST EARL OF PEMBROKE: GILBERT DE CLARE

Strongbow his followers called him because of his enormous strength
and extra long arms that joined together with a Welsh longbow could
split a Saxon helmet at 300 yards. It was even whispered that it was
Strongbow's arrow that had magically pierced the Saxon King Harold's
eye that day at Hastings turning a route into a Norman victory. Gilbert
De Clare was one of the most formidable warlords in feudal Europe.
With the misty power of Otherworld Celtic magic added to his knowledge of Arabian alchemy, his power was as frightening at midnight as
it was at noon on the battlefield—feared by friends and enemies
alike.

How Lord Gilbert had succeeded in isolating the Welsh city of
Pembroke and establishing it as an outpost for his family of Norman
invaders remained his secret, but it was known he had befriended
one Bledri, chief Druidic bard in the court of the Welsh prince of
Dyfed. Bledri had been trained in the oral history of his people as
well as the ancient knowledge of the power of the rhyme. It was said
that a Celtic rhymer had within him the power of heaven and earth
and could bring about the downfall of even a powerful king if that

king were to become headstrong and forget his proper role in the service of his people. But even more importantly, Bledri's training had also contained the legends of Arthur and his knights and their pursuit of the Grail. These legends had captivated the Norman conquerors and spread throughout the courts of France and Italy. And although their Catholic priests and bishops had attempted to remake the Grail Chalice into a Christian allegory of Christ's passion and death, the pagan meanings of the Grail had taken root within the new Norman aristocracy.

No one had embraced these pagan meanings more deeply than the Earl of Pembroke and his King, William Rufus of England. Together these men had immersed themselves into the deepest pools of Europe's esoteric knowledge and with the addition of the purest of Grail lore they had come upon a startling conclusion. According to the tales of Bledri, chanted by the fires at the castle keep in Pembroke—the numerical cycles of history that had elapsed since the beginning of time were about to spiral out in the year 1100. Should the appropriate sacrifices not be undertaken and the appropriate talisman's recovered from obscurity by the August celebration of Lugh—the Celts ancient the god of light—it was a certainty that the world as it was known to them and that time itself—would end.

Pope Urban's appeal for a Crusade to Jerusalem to reclaim the holy land where Christ was born had been only a clever ruse to draw the powerful barons into a common terror. For while the noble courts of Europe publicly professed their allegiance to the one true church of Rome, their secret knowledge of the Babylonian origins of their faith gave them a truer understanding of the Crusader's quest.

As a member of the Black Nobility, descendants of the Babylonian keepers of the darkest knowledge of human creation, Gerald of Windsor was one of these men. And so it was no surprise that when Strongbow decided to add Jerusalem to his list of conquests, King William Rufus had dispatched Gerald as his guide and guardian of the hidden secrets.

As I sat staring into the campfire, sharing scraps of food with the other Crusader knights while trying to blend the past with what was now clearly the present, I understood clearly the role that Gerald of Windsor played to Strongbow and realized for the first time that my dream and Gerald's were somehow the same.

"You look distant, Gerald," Strongbow said as he reached into the fire for a smoking scrap of meat, his piercing eyes bearing down on me, impatient for answers. "And what does your Geraldine dream tell us now?"

"We must locate the missing stones and bring them to the Red King." I said.

Gilbert laughed. "Red King. Huh! And what will Rufus do with them that we cannot do ourselves."

"Die for us, as he was chosen to do. Prophecy foretells that time is running out. Our lady demands a sacrifice."

Gilbert's eyes rolled at the mention of the name while his anger rose.

"Our queen Semiramis is an ogre whose appetite for the blood of men is endless."

"Then best she dine on Rufus, than dine on all of us."

Gilbert seemed shaken by my remark, almost distrustful of me. I had to reassure him that despite his arcane wisdom, the treasures we sought here in Jerusalem would be best brought home to the King than used to further advance Strongbow's already significant powers.

"I have spent much time in contemplation of the old books before leaving Rome—the books of Sumer, Akkad and the Chaldeans. What we must achieve by retrieving the stone is beyond what can be expected of mortal men. But if we can return to England in time, the King and all the sacred Kingdom can be saved."

Gilbert paused, then grunted reluctantly in agreement. "Then indeed King Rufus will have the stone my brother . . . as we have all agreed is wise."

I could feel Gilbert's resentment oozing from every pore in his huge frame. Gilbert wanted those stones and the power that went with it for himself. We had come a long way to the gates of Jerusalem and there was no telling how much further we had to go. But there was much to learn about the powers we were seeking. Contained within the ancient stones were the very powers that had brought life to earth and kept it here and without the authority of a powerful King like Rufus we were all in danger of losing more than just our souls. What the oracles and the old books told us was that we, as a race of men were in danger of losing the very ground in which our souls dwelt and that should we fail in our quest—our souls and the souls of all those who had gone before would be cast into the abyss. The consequences of failure were the complete and utter annihilation at the hands of a dark queen we could barely comprehend.

I drifted away from the campfire and back to the walled fortress. If Gilbert was as powerful a wizard as he seemed he would open the walls and if he could not, I would await the opportunity to arise. As the cock crowed to announce another day, I found myself again drawn to the water gate. But as the women scrambled to fetch their jugs of water I was greeted by a familiar stranger.

"You must help me," the woman said desperately, a pair of blue eyes peering from behind the veil. "Your army grows larger by the day. Inside the fear grows. Soon the soldiers will attack and there will be many deaths."

It was the veiled woman from the morning before, the one I'd saved from being molested. "There is little I can do for you." I told her, motioning to the field of tents and banners that stretched out behind us as far as the eye could see. "You should know that."

"I know that you have been sent by God. An angel dressed in black came to me in my dream."

"An angel, or a demon?" I replied.

The woman shook her head, growing distraught. "I come as a messenger from inside the walled city. My family. My sisters and their husbands, my father and mother have chosen me to bargain for their safety. They fear they will all be killed when the army of outsiders attacks. Vow to me protection for my people and I will take you to the secret you have come all this way for."

"And how would you know what I have come here for?" I asked, drawn to the strength in the woman's blue eyes.

"My family are Jews. My father, the priest of the Temple. These are things which can be seen . . . if you know how."

"Then since I can hold no secrets from you, you know that I cannot vow for these men. And I cannot protect you from what is to come."

"Then you can vow to try." She said. "Because if you cannot, then all you see, even the future itself is lost."

Her words struck the only chord that could reach me. This women in the veil with the blue eyes was my way into Jerusalem and whether I trusted her or not I had to do to whatever she asked.

"Yes. I vow."

"Then meet me here when the full moon crosses the bell tower," she said, pointing to the highest point on the city walls. "Meet me here and I will take you inside the walls."

***

I reported to the tall red-headed Earl of Pembroke as he met with a variety of Islamic merchants in his tent. I hadn't noticed the night before, but in the daylight Gilbert's long arms and delicate, almost womanly features were obvious. Lord Strongbow was neither entirely man nor woman but a practicing alchemist whose goal was to achieve a spiritual transformation and today he was attempting to acquire the means to complete his task.

"Ah, Gerald. Now here is the man who can tell me whether the stone these greedy merchants offer me is of the authentic variety or no."

I took the sphere of dark blue stone flecked with gold from Strongbow's hand, knowing what Gilbert wanted. Lapis Lazuli, true Lapis from the mines in Badakshan was of immense value whose esoteric power was well known. Most, if not all the rituals of Egypt, Babylon and Chaldea utilized the stone because it was said its use governed life and rebirth. The Egyptian priests had adorned the

Pharaoh's death mask with it—while the Israelites believed it was the material of God's throne. The oldest Sumerian texts, safely guarded at the archives in Rome maintained that lapis was the mystical stone of—Isis-Semiramis-Mary—the great mother of creation herself. And that by grinding it into a blue pigment, whatever words were written with it or whatever form it was used to describe would become manifest as creation.

I turned it toward the sun and examined it before the nervous fakirs as Gilbert watched. He wanted the magic elixir that would give him the power over birth and rebirth—the power to take his own life from the chances of fate and choose his own destiny. He wanted the stone. But even more, he wanted it to be real.

"Is it a sacred stone?" Gilbert asked, growing impatient.

I stared at the holy men, causing them to avert their eyes. The sale of holy relics was a big business for these men who'd grown wealthy on the gullibility of the faithful. A nod from me and they would be wealthier still. A no and they would be lucky to escape with their lives.

"It is a clever fake my lord. Indigo dye, ground carefully and mixed with fools gold with precision from old techniques. A beautiful artifact—but not sacred." I said, as I dropped the stone to the floor and watched it shatter.

"Take them," Gilbert said to his men as he crunched the rock beneath his foot. "And escort them from the camp."

Gilbert's soldiers grabbed the merchants by their beards and roughly led them from the tent. They were fortunate to live, but they would not leave the camp as they came. Gilbert's men were ragged and hungry and the merchants were rich and well fed. It was almost certain by the time they next saw their homes they would be relieved of all but the cloth covering their loins.

Gilbert was visibly disappointed. "How did you know?" He asked, sinking back in his chair as the protests of the fakirs faded in the distance.

"The Arabs construct their forgeries from tales and stories of the sacred stones, not the real things. The Jews were their caretakers. When Babylon was destroyed its inhabitants fled to the four corners of the earth. But the Jews came here. If anyone knows of their whereabouts and their true powers, it would be them."

"So how do we reach them?"

"The Jews have already reached me."

I told Gilbert of my meeting with the woman and her promise.

"And what does she wish in return?"

"Safe passage for her family and her people." I offered.

Gilbert's eyes widened at the thought.

"That's all?" He said.

"And my vow to protect her." I added.

"Then as I swear by St. Dionysus. She shall have it," he declared.

I stared carefully at the man William the Red King had sent me to watch over. Gilbert was a ravenous, independent and merciless Anglo-Norman. But then, so was every other follower of William Rufus. What made Gilbert different wasn't his hunger, but what he was hungry for. He was a man to whom the acquisition of spiritual power was the single most important reason for the adventure to Jerusalem and it was clear he would risk any earthly power to get it.

He would have to be watched and held to his bargain, that was, of course if I wasn't killed the moment I set foot on the other side of the wall.

That was the thought that preoccupied me all through the day and into the warm Jerusalem night. But there was little I could do now to avoid my fate.

As I left the encampment under cover of darkness and headed through the smokey camp fires, I wondered about the woman and her promise. What was she like with those blue eyes behind the veil— and why did the Black Knight choose to visit her. What shadowy plot was he orchestrating with these dreams.

My thoughts broke off as the woman arose from the cistern and drew me by the hand down into the darkened tunnels beneath the city. The steps were slippery and wet, water collecting in the deep depressions of untold millennia of footsteps, splashing like a thousand voices as rats scurried past our feet. Above was the ancient city. So much had happened here it made my head spin. But we continued on until we emerged into what seemed a torch-lit subterranean grotto and a small handful of men and women huddled next to a winding stairwell.

"This is my father," the woman said, motioning toward an elderly man who was obviously the high priest of the temple in his long blue robe and miter-like hat covered in silk. "And these are my sisters and their husbands," she added, pointing to two middle aged couples trying to calm a small, old woman who babbled excitedly.

"And this is my mother," she said as the little woman raised a finger and shook it at her accusingly. "She has come to curse whoever I have chosen to deliver us to safety."

I couldn't take my eyes off the little female figure as she swayed back and forth frantically, moaning and spitting in a high pitched screech. She was unhappy with me, but then she seemed unhappy with everything and she was sparing no one the venom.

"Enough of this!" The high priest pronounced as he raised his arm toward the stairwell and ordered the group upstairs. "The decision is made."

Instantly, the group moved up the stairs, the woman's mother pausing to issue one last unintelligible edict before being pulled away by the others against her will.

"My father will deliver to you what I've promised." The young blue eyed woman said, casting a long look at me before hurrying up the stairs. "I know you will be pleased."

The chamber was silent now except for the distant splashing of the water. And as the old man slowly approached, his feet hesitantly scraping along the damp stone floor, I realized he was blind.

"Of all the men camped at our gates, my daughter has chosen you to engage in this transaction," he said in a frail voice as his hands explored my face. "She has the gift of sight."

"Your wife protests." I answered, looking into eyes that were nothing but a smear of yellowish white.

"My wife thinks it is only she who is capable of making wise choices and she was not allowed to choose you. Unfortunately, she does not value the spiritual currency of these invaders," he said raising an eyebrow. "I assume my daughter does?"

The man tensed, his ear turning towards me so as not to miss a whisper.

"I have made the arrangements." I told him, hoping the old man couldn't hear the pounding of my heart as it nearly jumped out of my chest.

"With who?"

"Lord Gilbert de Clare. Earl of Pembroke."

"De Clare," the old man mumbled, trying to remember. "Yes. Yes. He is known to me," he said excitedly as he knelt forward, sinking his hands into the gravel floor. "We shall begin."

I felt awkward as I watched him bend to the ground. I even felt compelled to mimic him, only to be surprised as his frail hands drew back a hunk of flat rock.

It was a trap door that led into a deep cavity and as I followed the old man down the crude slippery steps, I began to feel the pull of some irresistible force.

"And now you will understand from where dreams come," the high priest said, feeling his way.

The path was totally dark and I clung to the old man's robe. But as we emerged into a broad, high ceilinged cavern, light seemed to glow from all around us.

Then as the old man led me toward what resembled a huge, egg-shaped stone with a hole cracked open at one end, I realized I had found the secret I had come for. "The Bible is written in a code within which all things are told and all futures foreseen," the old priest said, as he led me toward the partially cloaked shell which glowed with the brightness of the sun from dozens of smooth golf ball-size, crystals of various colors.

"Not only the letters but the sounds and the arrangements of the columns themselves are ways for understanding God's intentions. As you look into the glowing gems you will see how material is gathered and formed, shaped and fashioned into life. But there is only one true path that fulfills our creator's intent of illumination and that can only be achieved when perfect harmony is achieved."

I marveled at the sight. It was almost as if each crystal in its way represented a universe and within that universe were millions upon millions of possibilities, each one as accessible as the other. The light seemed to hum through each of them in a different tune and as I held my hand over them their music seemed to reach out to me. The high priest spoke. "The language of the ancients was a language of mathematics containing certain numerical correspondences that when achieved, reveal that God's plan has been fulfilled. Each of these stones plays a part. Each stone fulfilling a unique quality in God's plan." The old man whispered. "I have seen God's Kingdom and heard his voice. I have dedicated my life to understanding his mysteries. Are you prepared to do the same?"

As I whispered my replay, "yes" the old man sank to his knees, intoxicated by the sounds and colors that seemed to swarm around him and then he began to chant.

"The old religion treasured the power of words. In light these words brought paradise and pleasure. In darkness these words spell malice and deceit. Free us from the darkness now. Free us to fulfill your wisdom and your blessing."

I felt an odd sensation as the old priest pulled the remaining cloak from the egg, unveiling the entire cache of stones. Then, as a blinding fusion of color and sound poured out around me I found myself consumed in a multi-dimensional swirl of images.

"Though the spheres give us the powers of creation," the old man said as he traced a pattern of circles connected by lines in the air, then filled each with a different color sphere, "the order of that creation must be carefully designed. For though he who possesses the spheres, possesses time itself, the order must be followed to the letter or all will result in chaos."

I stared at the glowing diagram, hypnotized by the bright colorful stones, stones only remotely similar to the one Gilbert had toyed with in his tent that morning.

I was mesmerized by them now. There was power in them, so much power I barely noticed the set of diamond shaped eyes in the long, dark, snake-like body that now seemed to close in around us.

***

Outside the city walls a handful of men climbed from the cistern and soaking wet, crept toward the long-armed Lord Gilbert, waiting nearby.

"We followed so he would not see," the first man said as he stood shivering in the cool night air. "The tunnels lead all over the city. With six, perhaps eight men we could unlock the city gates."

"And be in the city by morning," Gilbert said, his eyes combing the high walls.

"Yes, my Lord, easily." The man said.

Gilbert smiled a satisfied smile as he scratched at his long red beard. "Then alert the other barons. It's time to claim what we came for."

BLISS

Languid shapes rose from a gentle green lake, took form and wrapped themselves around me as I was lifted above the city in a cloud of light.

Housed in a serpent's egg and buried in the deepest recesses below the city, the spheres acted as crystal receivers, channeling the voices of the universe into my head.

I floated there, listening to the music, art and geometry before the gates of a white castle in the clouds when suddenly a woman appeared. Tall and blond in a long white dress, she stood—holding in one hand the reins of three huge black horses and in the other, a stone. It was the stone we had come all this way for, the blood red, pulsating gemstone and she had come to give it to me. It hung before me in the air, dancing out an invitation.

But as I reached out to take it for my own I snapped awake, and as I snapped awake, it dissolved into a thousand red sparks. Outside, Gilbert's men had overpowered the guards and unbolted the heavy wooden door, opening the holy city to the legions of Crusaders. But of all the thousands who poured through the gates, only Gilbert and I knew the dark secret of our quest.

Men stormed through, horses screamed and women fled, only to be cut down and dragged by the hair to their deaths. Old men, children, nothing mattered. The Crusaders were tired and possessed with God's vengeance. But not Gilbert.

As he entered the city he ignored the burning and looting and made straight for the Temple and the home of the high priest.

***

I was barely conscious when I heard the first sound of the cries. To me they were voices from far away. But as they grew louder I magically saw the Jewish family as they were dragged from their beds onto the rooftop of the Temple—the young woman shielding her face. I tried, but could barely move.

I was alone now, alone except for the stones. Like a powerful engine, they lay quiet, their brilliance diminished by the horror above, but only slightly. The woman had delivered them to me as promised and because of her father I knew even the meanings of their colors. The blue and green returned with me to their proper place would reveal to me the secret of eternal life. The red would give me control of it.

But as I reached out and held it in my hand, I realized something was wrong. In my delirium something dark and wet to the touch had encircled the egg and as I bent low through the cracked opening, I came face to face with its guardian—the serpent.

Even before the pain had reached my brain, I could feel my arm swelling from the poison of the hideous serpent and as it filled me, I was filled with all the horror that lay above.

Sickened and confused I could barely remember climbing the darkened corridor or the wetness of the ladder as I fled the manifestation. All I sensed was the stench and the smoke that burned my eyes as I emerged on the roof of the Temple and saw the woman and her family surrounded by Gilbert and his soldiers.

"You vowed! You vowed" The woman screamed as she turned toward me, a look of absolute terror in her eyes. I ran toward her. I would explain that I had not meant to betray her. But there was no time. "I curse you and yours," she said as she reached beneath her torn shawl and withdrew a dagger, then with one quick thrust, brought it down hard onto her own breast.

I stood alone on the rooftop searching for an explanation. But there was none. Why had the Black Knight brought me here to see this and why had he chosen this woman to deliver me?

"To remind you," the voice of the Black Knight answered as I turned to see myself reflected in his shimmering image standing atop the Temple. "Look into my darkness and see thyself. We are together again as it was intended from the beginning of time. Now you will know what I know. See what I see. And you will remember."

A sick feeling, distant but familiar swept over me as I peered at myself in the bloody rooftop pool of the Temple and I remembered my words to Alissa. I had finally met the Black Knight, the young Gerald of Windsor from a thousand years ago on his own terms, and I had discovered that he was no stranger. The Black Knight from my dreams, the image haunting me in the mirror was my own.

"Don't you love me the best?" He said.

I closed my eyes and tried to say no, but the words refused to come out.

THE
CONNECTION

I was still screaming when I awoke on the floor staring into the eyes of the little old Anglican church rector in his white collar and gray jacket, my arms clapped across my chest in the stony repose of a Crusader.

"I thought I'd lost you." The rector said, a look of concern rippling up his forehead in a series of deep wrinkles.

"What happened to me?" I asked, as the gentle little man helped me to my feet.

"I'm not really sure," said the rector, staring at me suspiciously. "I found you here, lying next to the stone effigies of our Crusader Knights. You were so cold and gray, for a moment I even thought you were one of them."

I struggled to my feet. "I was one of them. They asked me to join them. They were in black and the nuns were over there reading and . . . effigies?" I looked at the stone gray knights with their legs crossed in the Chi-Rho symbol. My mind was spinning. "Where am I?"

The rector peered over his glasses. "Why the Inner Temple, of course. The home of the Knights of the Temple of King Solomon. The design was intended to mimic the real Temple of Solomon with its circular dome. How they knew that I don't quite know, but it's said they discovered his secrets and brought them here."

"What kind of secrets?"

"Mostly things that would be taken for granted today I'm sure. Medical techniques, mathematical formulas, mostly mundane things."

"Mostly? They were deeply religious, weren't they? Maybe even mystical?"

The rector stammered, trying to avoid the question. Then spoke knowingly. "The most mystical of all the Knighthoods. The Inquisition accused them of all sorts of practices. But that was a long time ago."

"Exactly what kind of practices?"

He shivered as he stared over my shoulder at the assembled stone effigies, then whispered. "Perhaps we shouldn't talk about that here. Let's go inside the kitchen and have some tea."

***

The rector spoke as he rifled through a drawer of old papers. "The Knights Templar went off looking for the Holy Grail, the keys to eternal life and control of the material world. You won't read that in any conventional history book, but you must remember in 1117 Britain and most of Europe was a very pagan place. In fact some complain it still is. The people believed that nature gods and goddesses took and gave life and Judeo Christianity or no—they had to be appeased."

"1117? The first Crusade was in 1099 wasn't it?"

"The Templars were not a part of the first Crusade, but arrived later on and set up at the ruins of the Temple of Solomon. Over time they adopted the Temple as their holy place and venerated the wisdom and practices of the Jewish King Solomon.

"Wherein lies their problem."

The rector looked at me defensively. "The Inquisition accused the Templars of worshiping idols, renouncing Christ and praying to human skulls that talked back," he said apologetically. "It's hard to know for sure what they really believed in because it was all confessed to under torture. But it seems they did practice much of the old religion. The men who organized the Crusade were very mystical people from royal families that extended back, long before the time of Christ. In fact it might be said that Christianity provided only a new mantle for their real pursuits which involved something very secret. What that secret was is often referred to as the Grail, but what exactly the Grail is, is still a mystery. All I can say is, it seemed to have been most concerned with sustaining life."

"After the end of time?" I asked, vaguely remembering my dream of Jerusalem.

"Some believe that. They certainly did. Church writings of the era around 1099 seem to suggest a deep fear that the end of time was at hand and that unless a holy Crusade was mounted to Jerusalem, time would run out. Perhaps this fear was unfounded, but the new Anglo-Norman royalty of William the Conqueror and his sons, took the Celtic religion very seriously. It's believed William the Conqueror's son William Rufus, who died a year later, was actually the willing victim of a secret nature ritual to buy more time. According to the legend, the spilling of the divine king's blood was necessary to consummate the sacred marriage with the earth's mother goddess and maintain fertility. Presumably this old mother goddess liked her dose of ritual bloodletting and if she didn't get it, she cut you off. Anyway, whatever the Crusaders did in Jerusalem, or whatever they found, I guess Rufus succeeded in postponing the inevitable."

"So the Templars came along 17 years later and picked up on these pagan practices all with the approval of Rome?"

"Today these things would seem un-Christian and clearly heretical, but back then Christianity wasn't as clearly defined as it is today. The church had long advocated the worshipping of holy relics to attain favors—selling indulgences, exorcizing demons, speaking in tongues ... The early mass was vastly different than today and perhaps at times even wildly erotic. It wasn't until later that Rome clamped down, after they saw exactly how powerful the true knowledge of these rituals made the Templars."

"So what I saw were their ghosts, still searching for hidden secrets of the Grail after all these years?"

The rector seemed troubled. "No. You said the knights that greeted you were in black and that the women, the nuns were advising them on which volumes to consume?"

I nodded. "Yes."

"Then I do not believe your Black Knights are Templars in search of the Grail. I believe your black knights may be the guardians of it." He said, growing even more troubled.

I was confused. "So what does that make me?"

"The unenviable negotiator—between light and dark. Medieval mysticism is not my calling, nor are Celtic Grail legends. But there is a woman near SOHO who runs a shop," the rector said as he finally pulled a wrinkled card from the pile. "Ah, here it is. MARY UNDERHILL, ASTROLOGER TO THE ROYALS. Now she may be able to help you."

MAD MARY

The faded photos on the wall of the cluttered shop showed Mary Margaret Underhill to have once been an elegant woman. Now she was a large grey rabbit hopping from aisle to aisle in the old bookstore, sniffing and poking through the piles of books that littered the store.

"It's here somewhere, I know," she said as she disappeared in a dusty cloud only to reappear an instant later waving a thin dog-eared book, her glasses perched at the end of her nose. "HEEEEEEERE it is! **Strongbow's Conquest of Ireland**."

"Strongbow," I remembered the name.

"Yes. Strongbow," She said, blowing the dust off the cover and handing it to me. "A pet name for Lord Richard De Clare, Second Earl of Pembroke and son to the first Earl, Gilbert—Crusader, holy warrior and alchemist. Now, there was a team of Norman war horses. Both actually went by Strongbow for their expertise with the Welsh Longbow. Some say they were really both the same person. But either way they both shared the same dream of finding the Grail. Gilbert went to the Holy Land in 1099. His son Richard invaded Ireland in 1170. Apparently their expedition to Ireland got them into trouble because by then Henry II and his Templars were looking for it there too. The search drove everybody to war and nearly to ruin. Strongbow claimed Ireland for himself. Henry sailed to Dublin and confronted him, face to face. Strongbow backed down and the English and the

Irish have been fighting ever since. But if anyone got the Grail it was those Fitzgeralds. You did say your name was Fitz Gerald didn't you?"

"Yes." I answered, no longer completely surprised to hear that my dreams might have some historical basis.

"All the children of Gerald of Windsor and the Welsh Princess Nest are Fitz Geralds. Fitz is Norman French for son-of. There's so many now they're considered a race of their own. Anyway, it's them the book is about, but they all came to Ireland under Strongbow. Look in the back if you don't believe me. Look, looook! It's all there, plain as the nose on your face what they went to Ireland for."

I turned the pages of the delicate old book and read aloud."Genealogical Tables Of The Geraldines And Their Kinsmen, Legitimate Descendants of the Princess Nest, daughter of Rys ap Tudor, The First Adventurers In The Conquest of Ireland: **"Maurice FitzGerald, Reimund FitzGerald, Griffith FitzGerald, William FitzGerald** . . . **William Fitzgerald** was my father's name."

Mary smiled coyly as it sank in. "Go on."

"Milo, Alexandre, Gerald . . . the list is endless." I said.

"All sons and grandsons of the very first Gerald, Gerald the Crusader, keeper of the King's castle at Windsor. This was no ordinary expedition and no ordinary family. This was a holy undertaking, some might even say a homecoming for a family of priests and soldiers whose mother was a Celtic Princess, a GRAAAAAAIL PRINCESS. Nest of the Tewdor line."

"Grail Princess?

Mary squinted, remembering. "Indo-European traditions going back to Sumer and Babylon thousands of years ago. All that stuff about fertility rituals and sacred numerology, the divine king and the Hieros Gamos spread from there to Persia, the Middle East and Europe. It was the world's first universal religion because everybody did it. Everybody worshipped the source of life, the Grail, the matrix, mother of all things. If you wanted to learn the mysteries you went down to the temple where the local priestess taught you everything you wanted to know, and then some."

"So why is it secret now?"

"Copyright infringement! Everybody who comes along from Nebuchadnezzar on down wants the power of creation for himself—the magic rituals, the words of power. First it's the Pharaoh, then Sargon, then Solomon, Alexander, Julius Caesar and the Pope. Now it's Bill Gates and Rubert Murdoch hoarding the numbers and locking them up in little boxes, counting out their Shekels or Dinars or Pounds. But what are their qualifications for such wealth and power? And what do we get next? Gene splicing, bio technology, patented organ replacement? Once you've reduced a human being to a series of numbers inside a laboratory computer ... where are we then? We're not supposed to live here forever, not like this."

I stared down at the book. "And what have these guys got to do with all that?"

"Everything," Mary said, growing darkly serious. "And you owe it to yourself to know the truth—the truth about the past and the truth about your place in that past."

"That's why I'm here. I need your help. I can't figure this out on my own."

Mary smiled. "Then come with me," she said taking me by the arm and leading me toward the back room. "There is a purpose behind the meaning. Let me show you what it is. And don't you worry. I won't bite. Not unless you want me to!"

THE BOARD OF DESIGNERS

Lord Gilbert sat silently at the huge antique round table of the Transitron board room, listening carefully as an uneasy Rick Kendall faced fifteen of Britain's most successful venture capitalists.

"My investigation into the interference problems have so far turned up little hard evidence to support the IRA theory."

"It must be them," a middle aged man with huge, grey whiskers—Lord Edmund DeBurgo—said as he tapped his finger disapprovingly. "Those Irish types are born terrorists. Should have moved the lot of them off the island when we had the chance."

"The minister for State Security agrees," Rick replied politely. "But my own inquiry indicates the problem originates somewhere internally."

Rick's revelation rattled the other board members.

"But we've spent millions on new equipment and the interference is world-wide." Lord Randolph Montgomery said, alarmed.

"And so are we. Lord Randolph, it's the new frequencies. The electronic web encircles the globe to an extent it never has before. Unlike just a few years ago we're now living in an electronic world." Rick said. "The speed of the computers, the distances involved may have created a qualitative Doppler effect. We've somehow pushed beyond the laws of physics."

Lord DeBurgo inquired further. "You mean we're reaching some kind of threshold?"

"I'm saying we may have crossed it." Rick said, as he reached for an envelope and pulled out a handful of clippings, then handed them around the table. "December 22, 1992. The U.S. Federal Communications Commission was called to investigate a jamming of police radios in Pennsylvania."

Another board member squinted as he picked up the paper and assumed the role of town crier. "An intensive search revealed the problem was a $20 electronic Christmas ornament playing on a woman's mantle piece?"

"April of 94," Rick continued. "Airline carriers in the U.S. ban radios, CD players and video games due to spontaneous and uncontrollable malfunctions in their aircraft's flight control systems."

"Don't tell me you're trying to blame us for crashing airplanes." DeBurgo said, snidely curling the end of his mustache with his fingers.

The room filled with laughter as Rick tried to make his point.

"They don't know who to blame. But the problems are getting more common and much to frequent. Something's happening with the electronics. We're picking up signals from somewhere but we don't know how or even what they are. We're in over our heads. Our new Dream Catcher is proof of that. We've opened a door on another dimension gentlemen—a dimension as deep and wide and frightening as the human mind. We have no idea where it leads or how to control it."

DeBurgo insisted on minimizing the danger. "These are sensitive technologies with profound abilities, I grant you. Our new Dream Catcher technology has produced some peculiar effects. But having our test subjects project their own fantasies before them in 3 dimensions is an unexpected technological bonanza."

Rick held firm. "Our test subjects have not only found themselves projecting dreams out of their own heads Lord De Burgo, they've found themselves projected into other people's dreams as well."

De Burgo glared. "Meaning?"

"Meaning, they became trapped in someone else's dream, or world or universe or whatever you want to call it. This might be fun if we knew how to control it, but we don't. Under normal conditions, the borders between my dreams and your dreams or my dreams and consciousness are not a problem, but if our technology somehow breaks down the borders and mixes them up, I don't know where that process ends."

"Is nothing sacred?" Montgomery said sarcastically, raising an eyebrow.

"Precisely," DeBurgo said, leaning down and focusing an intense glare at Rick. "And that's why this fellow's dream book is so damned important. Did you get us a copy of it yet?"

Chilled, Rick's face dropped. "No. He won't part with it."

"Mr. Kendall. We need a copy of that book," a third board member, Sir Sidney, pressed. "We need a copy of it now."

The room went silent as Lord Gilbert, content to listen, suddenly rose from his chair and walked to the window overlooking the Thames.

"I think Sir Sidney has made a very good point," he said stretching his long arms out in front of him until they spanned the entire length of the window. "We've bought that book and we want it here. You should use whatever means are necessary to acquire it."

"I'm doing what I can," Rick said, addressing Lord Gilbert directly as the other board members went silent.

Lord Gilbert turned, facing the group for the first time. It was amazing, his likeness to Strongbow, his red hair, his long arms, but more than that, his intensity. There was an almost mystical quality about him and as he stretched himself up to his full height, Rick saw something in him for the first time.

"You said it, yourself Mr. Kendall. We have crossed a threshold. I designed those electronics and I've studied the reports. But that threshold is a crossroads for mankind. The world of wars, of bickering and fighting, of violence is done. The old goddess, that old blood-thirsty-hag-bitch queen of the night has been overthrown. Now a new dream is about to be born, an electronic dream that will tie the world together and open each person's mind to the next. What kind of world do you think it will be when we can't hide our secrets? A good one or a bad one?"

Gilbert leaned down into Rick's face, staring intently. "I think it's going to be a good one Mr. Kendall and as its caretakers my friends and I are very anxious to ensure that nothing goes wrong with the delivery."

THE TIME MACHINE

Mary's back room was a museum of Pre-World War II Britain, a time machine back to when London ruled a material world that seemed now to be only a dream.

Photographs of the Duke and Duchess of Windsor mingled with packs of Tarot cards and quartz crystals, easy days at the polo grounds with ladies in big hats and white dresses, seances by moonlight and secret romances. It was a fairly-tale world of fast cars, beautiful women and lavish expense that now existed only in memory.

"They were the jewels in the crown." Mary said as she gazed longingly at the pictures of an era long gone by. "But they were the last of the real kings. The Kingdom is no longer blessed. The spell has worn off, the magic is gone." She turned toward me, a look of sadness in her eyes. "Even the Norman invaders, those brutal men, knew about the magic and how to keep it. They scoured the earth looking for the secret, searching all the way to Jerusalem and back. And by the time Gilbert and Gerald returned to England a year after the Crusaders had conquered the holy city, the world was on the edge of a great cosmic change."

Mary placed the book at her finger tips and waved them over it as if drawing the story out into her hands. "The two had gone off to Jerusalem as allies, but Gilbert's alchemy and the cravings for power it produced had drawn them apart and events were to push them even further."

Mary's voice was hypnotic, growing more and more distant as it lead me back down the trail of time until I again found myself immersed in that summer of 1100, riding at the head of a long column of horsemen as we rode through the King's New Forest at Windsor.

The air was still and hot, the horses skittish as if sensing some unseen presence. Gilbert was much changed in the one year since Jerusalem. Freakish and old beyond his years with one side of his face quite female, the other covered in patches of red beard, he could barely cling to the saddle. I felt changed as well. Dressed in the armor of the Black Knight I felt a keen sense of detachment—hardened and cold almost as if my heart had been struck from my body.

"I've traveled far enough," Gilbert said as he reached weakly into a saddle bag for yet another magic elixir. "The flames are consuming me and yet I freeze."

"Then I shall go on without you," I said, feeling a rising contempt for Gilbert whose betrayal in Jerusalem I could not forgive. "We are nearing the green chapel and the hour approaches."

We had raced from Jerusalem to Rome then overland to Marseilles for our return to England and our a rendezvous with the King at the New Forest—away from the courtiers and prying eyes of the castellans and seneschals. We had come to fulfill our promise by presenting him with the means to ensure the life of the Kingdom. The red stone in the hands of the true king would inaugurate a new era for the Kingdom as well as all mankind and no one but Rufus, son of the Conqueror William I, could provide that sacred role. But the sudden cawing of the ravens and the swift beating of hooves stood warning there was danger to our plan and as I hastened my approach to the old, abandoned chapel I could see that our appointed hour and the opportunity it presented, had passed.

I rushed to the body lying under the elder tree and saw the one thing I feared the most—the Red King.

"By the face of St. Lucca, I've bought you time" he said, a broken arrow protruding from his chest. "But beware my brothers Henry and Robert. They are not of us."

I couldn't hold back the tears as I forced the stone into his bloody hand. It glowed for one brief moment and it seemed its aura would bring him new life.

"I have made arrangements for you to marry the Princess Nest at Dyfed," he said. With her, your mission will be complete.

"The Princess Nest is your brother Henry's concubine your majesty."

"The Princess Nest is an heir to a long past and a promise for the future that Henry's bastard's shall not rule. I have chosen you to carry that future. Repair to her family in Ireland who are aligned with us and when the time is right, the stone can be returned to its rightful home."

I watched helplessly as the king departed, eyes wide, legs bent in the awkward sign of the Chi-Rho. The last rays of sun faded and as the darkness grew a rejuvenated Lord Gilbert slowly rode up from behind.

"He's dead? So soon? The king is dead?" he asked.

"Because of you, you idiot."

Eager to shed blame Gilbert rose tall in the saddle. "It was Tirel who killed him. I saw him ride away."

"Tirel killed him because we were a day late. And we were a day late because of your greed and avarice. Had we returned in time a heaven's reward awaited us. Now we must spend a millennium fighting for our lives."

I removed the stone, now dripping with the King's blood and held it up for Gilbert to see. "On this stone is the blood of a new Kingdom and our claim to the Grail. Now go. Fetch the bearers before night fall. I shall ride to Winchester and welcome the new King."

Under Gilbert's instructions, Rufus' body was loaded onto a cart and hauled to Winchester—sacralizing the ground with his blood along the route. But the Red King's older brother Henry had little use for sacrifice. As he set his eyes on his new Kingdom, he set out to use the Red King's edict to inflame Gilbert's jealousy.

L

***

Nest had been taken as a hostage during one of Gilbert's early forays into Wales and was kept in London to ensure her father's allegiance to the crown. As fair and beautiful as a wild rose, she had quickly become the lover of the King's brother Henry and had produced—according to the new Norman order of law—a bastard, Fitz Henry. Now that he was King, Henry had the pick of the garden and would produce bastards as he pleased. Losing a mistress to the faithful servant of his brother was of little concern. Sending a royal baby-maker with the potential to make rivals back into Gilbert de Clare's armed territory was. Henry had to divide Gerald and Gilbert and keep them divided.

"And so in reward for his loyalty to my brother and to help keep my Welsh possessions securely from the Welsh," Henry said, drunkenly spilling his wine over the exposed breast of his freshest concubine. "I give my faithful and dangerous servant Gerald my favorite bitch-in-heat Nest, Princess of Wales. May he enjoy the fruits of her womb as much as I."

Gilbert stared angrily as two of Henry's voluptuous cast-offs tried to sooth his ego, but he brushed them off. Losing Nest meant nothing personal to Gilbert. Losing the Grail did. The new King had unwittingly let the nursery slip away into Gerald's hands, now Gilbert would have to find a way to get control of it, even if it took a millennium.

***

Instead of prosperity, the years in Pembroke following the Crusade saw a decline in the family of the great Lord Gilbert. Torn between protecting his possessions in Normandy and dabbling deeper and deeper into his alchemy, Lord Gilbert and his look-alike son Richard found themselves in trouble with the Crown.

Over the years, the new English King Henry II and his Templar, Grail Knights had grown knowledgeable about Jerusalem and increasingly suspicious of the De Clare's ambitions. Being no stranger to the powers of the nature rituals, Henry had annexed their lands in Normandy. Thus deprived, Gilbert's son Richard had become a desperate and a jealous man.

Having grown up fighting side by side with Gerald's children, he knew the sons of Nest and Gerald as brothers. He also knew of their unusual abilities, where they would often think and act as one. As their lord, the growing horde of Geraldine knights were still subordinate to Strongbow, but as the descendants to Gerald and a Welsh Princess—they outranked his pedigree and this more than anything infuriated him.

Strongbow's jealousy for Nest's young grandson William was particularly keen. Of all Gerald's issue, William seemed to possess the fire within that burned the brightest and as the old woman's voice echoed through the Great Hall at Pembroke on a cold winter's night, he could barely keep himself from spying.

"You are the fruit of the prophecy. As the old Merlin foretold, the product of two races, Norman and Celt, destined to return the Grail to its rightful home," Nest in toned as she sat by the hearth, her young grandson William by her side.

Her eyes searching the darkness beyond, she withdrew a gilded box from under the chair and placed it in her lap. "But the darkness hides its secret until the time is right. Cherish it, believe in it with all your heart and you will pass its legacy on to your sons to be revealed to you at the end of time."

"But grandmother. How can I be there at the end of time when I am here with you now," the young William asked. Nest opened the box and withdrew the luminous red stone and held it before the fire.

"That too you will understand through a new miracle. But until then there is much to learn," she said as tears welled in her eyes. "As it was seen by the prophet Daniel, with this stone unmade by human hands, you have the power to conquer death and create a kingdom that will never be destroyed. But to do so requires great wisdom and the conquest of your darkest fears. To use the power of the stone now without the conquest of those fears would be fatal not just to you, but to the world that is to come."

Nest placed the stone in the young William's hands and patted his head.

"Take this to Ireland, to where it will be safe. The arrangements have been made by your grandfather. When time has neared its end, the dreams will show you how to use it. Don't be surprised at what it asks of you. The trials will be many and sometimes seem impossible. But there will be help along the way. Take it when you can."

The sound of Strongbow's shuffling, ogre-like feet could be heard from behind the long tapestries but Nest chose to ignore them, focusing instead on her grandson who whispered a warning into her ear.

"And what if they are stolen by enemies?"

"Only the foolish would try," she bellowed loud enough for the figure behind the curtain to know he was revealed. "For, it only works for those it has chosen and destroys those it has not."

Exposed, the jealous Lord Richard, son of Gilbert stumbled onto the floor, red faced and angry at having been caught.

"More dangerous are those who would keep you from your goal." Nest said, as she pointed a finger and leveled it hard in his direction. "For it is they who do not understand the nature of the gift."

***

As if in a dream, I found myself distracted by the jangle of a bell and as I turned back toward Nest, found Mary pausing before she raced to the front door of her shop. "If you are in need of further answers as to why Rufus should place such confidence in your stock, I would suggest a visit to the British Museum and the remains of the bogman from Lindow Moss. I think you'll find that what Strongbow had been seeking, the Geraldines became. And speaking of Geraldines, I think there's someone here who's been looking for you."

The sound of Alissa's voice brought me back to reality.

"Dad, finally!" She said, as I emerged into the storefront.

"What's the big deal?" I asked as I noticed someone awkwardly skip behind a bookcase.

"Big deal?" Alissa said, staring at me with a bewildered look. "You've been missing for three days."

My head spun again. "What?"

"Nobody's seen you since you walked out of Transitron," she said as Rick peered out almost playfully from behind a shelf. "If it hadn't been for Rick we'd never have found you at all."

My blood went cold. "So how did he find me when nobody else could?" I said as I grabbed Alissa and hurried her outside.

"He was just trying to help." Alissa said as I pulled her past Rick and onto the rainy Soho street.

"Take help from a man like that and you're asking for trouble."

"Dad, please!" Alissa demanded as I hailed a cab. "I was worried. He was the most logical person to go to and I was right. He found you."

The look on Alissa's face calmed me down. "I'm sorry. You did the right thing," I told her, "But the next time something like this happens, call the police, not him."

Alissa smiled as we stepped into the dry, black London cab and drove off, leaving Rick to soak up the rain. He'd been lucky that she had come to him for help and he knew it. Rick wanted that book more than ever and over the last few days Gilbert had been coming down even harder than usual on him to get it. He'd pulled out the stops to find me. But it had been Lord Gilbert's mention of the Templar Church that had clued him in and it was this that made him suspicious.

There was something going on here, something that he didn't understand. He knew that if he was ever going to find out what it was, he'd have to find a way into my life. And as we drove away, I knew by the look on Alissa's face which route he would be taking.

REUNION

I found myself lost in thought as the cab wound its way through the busy London streets and down by the Thames.

"You've never done anything like this before," Alissa said, her eyes searching aimlessly for clues. "Where did you go?"

"I'm not sure. It was just as if I was drawn into a . . . . " Just then I remembered the Dream Catcher aggie I'd pocketed at Transitron.

"What is that?" Alissa asked as I held it up to the light.

"I'm not exactly sure. Driver, take us to Bloomsbury Square."

"Where are we going?" She said, startled.

"The British Museum. I have to see something before we get home."

***

I began to feel the shift even before we reached the steps of the Museum. My dreams, if that's what they were, were expanding my knowledge of the past—bringing entire lifetimes into my consciousness for me to rerun like an old movie. Each time I lived one, I experienced a different part of a huge puzzle expanding from a dark purpose that I thought began with Rufus, Gerald and Strongbow 900 years ago.

But as Alissa and I turned the corner I realized my involvement in this had begun a lot further in the past than I could have imagined.

"It's you. I mean you and your brother and your mother. He looks like all of you." Alissa said as we stood before the rotating bust of an iron age man with dark hair and blue eyes.

"That's just a recreation of what he looked like." A guard said as he ambled over. "The real one's in that case over there. Sacrificed he was, bled to death to fertilize the earth."

Alissa seemed bothered by the image. "Why?"

"Because the alternative was far worse." I added.

Both Alissa and the guard looked at me strangely, but they seemed to sense I knew something more, something dark and purposeful about the murdered man. But they said nothing.

✳✳✳

The ride home was quiet, the evening clear and crisp until we passed St.Paul's and caught a glimpse of the huge Millennium Wheel on the other side of the river.

"I still think it's funny they built that thing for the Millennium celebration and couldn't finish it in time. You'd think with 1000 years to prepare . . . " Alissa said.

"I don't think they built it for the millennium. I think that was just an excuse." Alissa looked at me again, that concerned look in her eye but I couldn't explain. Worlds were rushing through my mind, lifetimes of images crisscrossing and crashing together. I'd crossed a threshold entering the Templar Church and since that moment my narrow, analogue view of life had been shattered. Afghanistan had been the beginning, but now I was actually living the world with new eyes and in more than one dimension. At any moment I felt I could slip away, drawn into the dream and perhaps never return.

"What's with the secrecy?" Alissa said, as she folded her arms across her chest. First you disappear for three days. Then I find you with this old rabbit of a woman who convinces you to rush off again to see a two-thousand year old murder victim who died to prevent something worse from happening? What's worse than being strangled and bled to death, not to mention being thrown in a bog?"

"Watching your world die, when you knew you could have prevented it."

"Are you talking about mom?"

"I'm talking about what your mom reconnected me to. I just realized I'd never have done any of it if it wasn't for her. That bog guy died to help his family keep something alive. His sacrifice was a ritual marriage—the sacred marriage—and your mother's sacrifice reawakened the understanding in me. Don't you see?"

Alissa shivered. "It's spooky, not to mention gruesome. What a waste of life."

"Who wouldn't risk a short stay here for a guarantee of eternal life at the end of time? That's what the Grail is Alissa. Winning the right to choose your own destiny forever. The real Grail."

Alissa seemed to understand for the first time. "You really believe there is such a thing?"

"I think that guy in the bog believed it not to mention at least one English King. Certain families keep the knowledge alive. That's why the Geraldines went to Ireland—because they found it again. And when they got there, they hid it. Eventually they probably forgot about it too."

"And this Black Knight? What's his role?"

"To make sure nobody else finds it."

***

It was late as I sat at my desk thinking about the last three days. But the more I remembered the less I wanted to sleep. In fact I felt as if I had been asleep all my life and now I was finally awakening. Though things had never been crazier they had never made more sense either. No one knew the human potential for creation or where that potential led. We barely understood what life was like in the past let alone anticipate what it would be like in the future. But as I opened the old book, *Strongbow's Conquest of Ireland*, I could feel the course of it all: the long buried voices, the prayers just waiting to be heard and as I turned the pages I knew I'd found the answer I'd been seeking.

WEXFORD, IRELAND 1170

It was the dream of the army on the beach, the one I'd had that last Sunday when I'd seen the Black Knight. But this one was written down in black on the yellowed pages of a book published in London in 1888 and it was no dream. It was history as recorded by the Geraldine priest Giraldus Cambrensis around 1188 added to the remnants of the ancient Celtic scholarship, known as the *Annals of the Four Masters*.

It was all there. Dermot, one of the many kings of Ireland had gone to Henry II in 1167 looking for help in regaining his Kingdom and Henry had foolishly sent him to the second Earl of Pembroke, Richard De Clare, to do the job.

Nicknamed Strongbow, Richard had relied on Gerald's son Maurice and their large family—now Christian mercenaries posted in the various courts of Europe—to do the dirty work. In no time, Maurice had won back Dermot's territory. In fact, according to the prelate Cambrensis, the Geraldine invasion of Ireland was nothing short of a holy miracle and as more Geraldines marched onto the beach under their family banner of the blood red X, it did seem they were destined to fulfill Merlin's Grail prophecy.

The Black Knight, Maurice's son William, swore himself to that purpose as he knelt on the beach with his brothers and cousins and uncles that morning in May 1170. Following in his grandfather's path, William had schooled himself in the art of Norman warfare. But as a member of the Black Nobility, William carried a spiritual weapon as well and when no older than a boy had accepted his grandfather's burden, his blackened armor and the dark spell that went with it. Nest had endorsed the enterprise reluctantly, realizing the invasion would wreak havoc on the last outpost of Celtic civilization. But seeing the dark clouds on the horizon, she knew the Grail could only survive under the protection of the Black Knight, hidden within its origi nal home.

William was a product of the two races of Norman and Celt. But he was also a member of a priesthood that stretched back all the way to Babylon whose own dark perseverance was dedicated to protecting the Grail and its secrets, no matter what. That mission smoldered within him, burned with coldness in all his brothers' hearts. But none burned with it so fiercely as the young chestnut-haired William. Wrapped in a leather pouch, he wore the luminous red stone over his heart, praying that it guide him to victory. But as he rode off the beach he knew that for now, it would be a long, long war.

The young woman hiding in the patch of yellow wildflowers knew it too and had come to help him. Who she was and why she'd taken such a chance William could not imagine, but as he dismounted and surveyed the flowers, his mind raced into the future. There was so much for him to learn and do, but he was not yet ready to face the power she represented.

William was prepared to kill for the Grail, but on seeing the girl named Siobhan rise from the flowers like nature itself, he was stopped cold.

In that split second he understood the meaning of the Grail. The Grail was life, embodied spirit with endless potential and here in Ireland it was everywhere. In that split second, his dual nature of holy warrior and Celtic Grail knight merged. He knew now what the Grail wanted. But he also knew that in the end, a great and wonderful dream would be fulfilled.

Siobhan was the incarnation of that dream, someone to help the Grail warrior through his impossible mission patiently waiting for him to arrive.

I thought about the dream on the beach that I had awoken from. Even through the pages of a hundred year old book, I could still feel Siobhan's message, the look of certainty on her face as the Black Knight froze before her.

It was easy for a Black Knight to kill without remorse. But to see the truth, smell the sweetness of the flowers as Siobhan stood in the sunlight, disarmed him. The Black Knight could fight any enemy but he could not fight life-itself, Siobhan would make sure of it.

She watched as he mounted his black horse and rode away, knowing she would see him again.

William, the grandson of the Holy Crusader, Gerald of Windsor and the Grail Princess Nest had come to Ireland with a mission and Siobhan would ensure he would learn all that was necessary to complete it.

THE ANCIENT KINGDOM OF OSSARY

Strongbow's Conquest read like it had been written yesterday, the twelfth century words and phrasing bearing none of the high-brow circumlocution English literature would later become famous for. Geraldus Cambrensis had intended it that way, stating in his preface that he intentionally avoided "courtly" language because it disguised the true meaning and intent. This decision had made him many enemies at court but despite perennial attempts to discredit him, his detailed story was considered the best account of any historical event on record. As the tutor to Henry II's son, the infamous Prince John, he knew all the inside gossip and the backstairs goings on, but as grandson to the Princess Nest he was a loyal Geraldine. This fact alone would have made him suspect at court and it was a sure bet his warnings had helped his family to undo much of Henry's designs. But the priest Geraldus had a deeper mistrust of Henry than just his intentions for his family. The Angevins were heretics, active practitioners of the Cathar faith and with the Geraldines firmly aligned with Rome, the mutual distrust extended far beyond baronies and kingdoms and into the spirit realm. From the first day they'd arrived in

Ireland the Geraldines were marked as enemies of the English throne and as they marched further into the countryside the war intensified.

The "army" of Geraldines was small by most standards, even by those of 1170. Thirty men at arms, sixty horsemen clad in mail and three-hundred bowmen. But up against the ancient Irish city state of Ossary they presented a formidable enemy. With Dermot's five-hundred clansmen armed with captured Viking axes swelling the ranks as they forged along the rocky road, the force was one to be feared.

Siobhan watched from the bushes as William and his half brother Fitz Stephen, attired in heavy Norman armor greeted the wild eyed Dermot. To William and his family of mercenary knights, war was a business, but this war was different. Dermot had made promises to Strongbow and his Fitz Gerald vassals; grants of land, even the hand of his daughter and the Kingdom of Leinster. Here was a chance for the family to escape the feuding rivalries of the European courts, put down roots and establish for itself its own kingdom.

Dermot was obsessed with revenge and would have given anything to get it. To him, this war was deeply personal and intense—as unforgiving as the unseen ghosts of the Tuatha De Danaan that swarmed the battlefield.

Ossary was itself a thousand year old kingdom, an independent state within a state, never taken by any enemy. It was not beyond the King of Ossary to issue a mystical incantation himself, while its location—in the heart of a sacred grove of oaks surrounded by a swamp—made it virtually impregnable.

All through the day, the attack took a heavy toll on Dermot's men and only by feigning defeat did they finally draw the men of Ossary out into the open where the Normans could get at them.

It was the last attack by the men of the city, it was the last day in the history of an ancient kingdom and Siobhan shed a tear as she watched the men cut down in ambush, as if harvested in their own field. For a thousand years, even before the time of Christ the Kings of Ossary had bargained and cajoled, traded and fought their enemies, even fearsome Vikings to a quiet peace. Now in the fading light of one afternoon in 1170, as they charged from their protected enclave—in what they thought was victory—they were systematically run to ground and cut down by the Black Knight and his brothers.

Dermot relished the victory as their severed heads were served up to him; undeniable proof that he alone was the true king of Ireland. But it would never be. As Nest foresaw, the coming of the Grail warrior broke a spell that protected Ireland from invasion and it would soon be the end for Dermot as well.

But the end for Dermot was the beginning for the Geraldines and as they sat by the fire nursing the days wounds, the Black Knight prayed for relief of the pain that stabbed like a knife at his heart:

"Domineo Veniteo Sacramentum eo Deo."

A candle flickered from an iron post inside his tent while he prayed, his eyes closed, his voice hushed, blending with the sound of swords being sharpened for the next day's battle and the moans of the injured.

A cold, damp breeze caused the candle to flicker, then die as the camp was filled with the sound of thunder. Then from the heavens the sky seemed to open as out poured an army of phantom warriors, filling the air with the curses and shouts of a thousand ghostly soldiers.

Long haired supermen in capes and kilts poured from the sky and swept among the Normans, who staggered to their feet and slashed at the air, firing arrows that pierced nothing but their fellow soldiers. Siobhan watched as the half naked and blinded soldiers stumbled from their tents, searching for their weapons or fled to the bog as panic swept the camp. Campfires swirled and tents caught fire while a great whisper rose from the shadows of the old stone fortress, growing until the thunder seemed to rumble out the words.

"We are the children of the goddess Danaan and we have come to claim your souls," it said.

The cry awoke William from his trance. Something told him this enemy could not be overcome with swords or arrows. He knew these warriors had come looking for something. Maybe they could even sense the stone in its pouch concealed in the darkness. He calmly walked into the confusion of the camp. There he withdrew the blood-red stone given to him by his grandmother and held it aloft for all to see.

"I am the son of Maurice Fitzgerald, grandson of Gerald and Nest the princess of Wales and I have come to reclaim what is rightfully mine," he shouted as the phantoms swirled around him, their axe blades and spears flashing like lightning in the darkness.

A great cry rang out, accompanied by the clanging of swords as streams of color seemed to pass through the stone like a prism. And with a burst of brilliant white light, the phantoms were gone. An instant later the cold breezes lifted and the shouting died, leaving the soldiers to stare at each other in terror. What kind of strange enemy had they had encountered? What did it mean for their future?

But to Siobhan, who surveyed the scene from her hidden spot, it was a sign. As she ran excitedly through the damp bogs and heavy woods to tell her mother, she could barely contain her joy.

Her mother had no idea of the commotion as she burst through the door and threw herself upon her at the hearth.

"The man with the power of dreams is approaching," she said breathlessly, taking her mother's hand. "It is as the prophecy foretold."

"Then we must pray to St. Brigit for his deliverance," her mother said, staring into the dwindling embers as they knelt by the fire and blew into it softly.

The smoke danced as the women's hot breath teased it from the coals and in a moment, the fire turned to a roaring blaze, licking the sides of the stone hearth and warming the room with a bright orange glow.

"She will help," the mother said smiling at her daughter. "She will most surely help. But you must help him too."

The girl's eyes gleamed as she nodded her approval. She had known from the moment the Black Knight arrived on the beach that he was the object of prophecy, a man whose heart would play a role, the key role in the future of her people. What her mother asked of her was what she lived for, had lived for all her life. Now she would follow him until the moment was right and they would be together. She knew in her heart that moment would be soon.

THE ARCHERS OF FINGLAS

The days of the invasion turned to weeks as Dermot and his intruders ravaged the countryside. No longer content with just the kingdom of Leinster, Dermot now saw himself as the new king of a Ireland. But as his conquest spread, the hatred for him spread as well. Alerted to his plan, the entire country rallied against him, and it seemed the ancient mother goddess of the Tuatha De Danaan was rising against him as well. Nothing provoked an Irish ghost more than the sacking of a sacred place and as Siobhan watched the disrespectful soldiers approach the shrine to Brigit, she knew that the mother of the Irish gods would be waiting.

Like that first night at the old fort, the soldiers knew nothing of the elemental powers of the ancient Christianized Irish gods and suspected nothing as they shoved their way through the doors toward her sacred fire. But as Brigit rose from the dying embers, at first licking, then reaching out to them and surrounding them in fire, they understood.

Here in Ireland where the old ways were still believed, where the fairy rings and the stone monuments surrounded you everywhere you went, magic still ruled. Here, where the four elements of life retained the power of form, Brigit danced and teased and as she consumed the men in flame, they realized the meaning of the sacred fire.

Screams filled the air as two of the soldiers ran from the church, their faces burned black and as William approached he realized another test was at hand.

"I breathed on Brigit's fire. I breathed on Brigit's fire," the soldier babbled as he staggered down the road, unmindful of the Black Knight as he watched coldly from his black stallion.

William dismounted and walked to the stone archway that framed the church door. He'd heard the stories of the Celtic gods, the Tuatha De Danaan. His uncle Giraldus Cambrensis had traveled all over Wales for such stories and had even obtained an original copy of Merlin's writings, translating them to Latin from an ancient Celtic script. They had told of the nature spirits and how their powers extended far beyond the control of Christianity, but William had never imagined anything like this. Inside lay the body of a soldier, curled and shriveled, his face frozen into a tortured death mask while hovering above him floated the beautiful flame of Brigit, beckoning for William to approach.

"Don't you love me the best?" She said with a crackling voice as her fiery caress licked at William's boots.

William remembered the words. These were the same words his grandfather had heard that day in Jerusalem when his armor had smoldered and his heart had turned to black. This was the power of the elemental fire, the force behind the Grail he had come to Ireland to harness, and as he withdrew the stone from its pouch, she approached.

"I love nothing." William replied coldly, his eyes beginning to glow a soft yellow.

"Then I must teach you," Brigit spoke as a tongue of flame reached out over the dead body of the soldier.

Seconds later William emerged from the church, clutching his left arm and barking out orders, but he would speak to no one of what had happened.

"Tear it down," he ordered over the protests of some Irish clergy who had gathering over the commotion. "Tear it down and scatter the stones so that no one may enter this place again."

"By whose order? This is a Christian Church," a bearded elder yelled from the crowd.

"By the order of Strongbow, Earl of Pembroke." William said, as he watched his men rope the steeple of the simple stone church to the ground. William mounted painfully. He'd had many strange experiences since he'd first set foot on the beach at Wexford but now he understood the difficulty of the dual mission he faced.

As a Celt with shamanic powers, he knew the fullness of life in a way no other race of people could feel it, powerful and at one with the air, the sea, the earth and the fire. But as a Christian holy warrior in the armor of the Black Knight he knew he must resist these temptations and remain detached and aloof from feeling. His heart would have to be maintained; pure, cold and locked as if in the darkness of an empty room.

His head swam and he grimaced in pain as the smoke rose from the rubble. He had destroyed Brigit's ancient place of worship held over from the days of the ancient Danaan, but Brigit had kissed him with her flame and as Siobhan watched him ride off, she knew her fire would soon burn through to his forgetful and blackened heart.

***

William swooned in the saddle. A storm grew as night descended and as he pressed on into the dark, a cold rain poured down with the force of darts on him and his weary companions. The countryside seemed alive with the spirits of the dead and the further they pushed into the night, the more they seemed to reach out and encircle them.

The four elements conspired against them as trees snapped, rivers swelled and mud clogged their path. The entire countryside was threatening to swallow them up and inside William felt like death.

"Don't you love me the best," the storm seemed to whisper as it swirled around William's delirious head. "No," he screamed, haunted by the vision of Brigit hovering before him in the frightening storm, while she burned his insides with her fire.

But Brigit was not to be dismissed. And as Siobhan watched from the forest, the fiery dart struck with the full fury of a nature defiled. William saw nothing as the lightening flowed over him in waves, killing his black stallion and knocking him to the ground. He felt nothing as Siobhan rushed from the bushes and pulled him from the boiling mud, his armor sizzling like a hot griddle. She had prayed to Brigit for his deliverance and now as her fire burned through him, his heart opened to a deeper dream.

***

William felt beyond a sense of time. All he felt was sunlight and the face of Siobhan as she hovered over him like a protective angel. He was inside some kind of crystal egg, like the ones buried beneath the Temple of Jerusalem. It was a crystal ship, a mansion of dreams, dreams that conveyed the spirit of life through the sunlight. Somehow through this sunlight William had been called and it was this same calling that had driven his grandfather, the Crusader Gerald to Jerusalem. To William it seemed like magic, but now I realized it was more than that. Like some huge solar clock in the shape of an egg, this was a time machine. This is where William's and Gerald's and all the other Geraldines spiritual life had begun. It was a point of embarkation, the gate through which light transformed itself through the four elements, took on the Monad of form and became human life.

How it did that was through some science of crystals William could not yet comprehend, but as he staggered to his feet and stumbled outside the crystal palace into a frozen wasteland, he realized what his job as Grail warrior really was.

William's job was not just to conquer death, but to restore through his heart, the wasteland that had been lost and make of it a paradise. But only by shedding the protective armor of the Black Knight could that be achieved.

***

The Black Knight opened his eyes to the sight of Siobhan framed against the bursts of lightning, mortally wounded but at last realized to a purpose. "I remember." he mumbled, his armor still smoking from the white hot bolt.

"It's those bleeding daemons come again to steal our brother," the young knight Godobert said to his companion as they caught sight of Siobhan, showering William in Irish verses.

"It's the bleeding Irish witches," his friend DeMonteforte shouted back, as he swept the rain from his eyes. "Quick. Kill her before she drags his soul to hell."

The knights put spurs to their horses and galloped hard toward their friend, knives drawn. But Siobhan was waiting almost as if she could read their minds.

"Disarm yourselves and give me your horses," she said as they pulled up before her, her manner provoking a look of confusion.

"And who are you?" DeMonteforte growled as the storm seemed to close in around them.

"Siobhan. Daughter of Macarthaig and princess of Desmond. Do not threaten me, or I'll give the sign for my men to attack."

The two men stood, cowed by the woman's audacity as they stared around them into woods that only a moment before had seemed filled with demons.

"Maybe the woman is a witch," Godobert whispered. "But if she is telling the truth we are in no position to defend ourselves."

"So what do we do?" DeMonteforte replied loud enough for Siobhan to hear.

"The man has been harmed by an ancient spell. Only when this is removed can he begin to heal," she said as the two confused men shared a blank look. "Beyond this road is a village where there are wise women. We will take him there."

"And if we don't?" DeMonteforte demanded as he tried to position himself more comfortably, knee deep in muck.

"Then this man will not live beyond this night, nor will your lord, nor your king, nor even your country."

William groaned and babbled as blood trickled from his mouth.

"Strongbow will have our heads for consorting with witches." Godobert cursed, as he shook his head in disbelief.

"That's later. She will have our souls now, if we don't."

Cursing demons and the Irish weather, Godobert and DeMontefort cast off their knives and hoisted William onto a horse, then as Siobhan took the reigns they slogged over the hill to a nearby village.

***

William lay unconscious on the table as the women assembled in the village Great Room to see what Siobhan had brought them. One by one they came and circled around the body, carefully observing the white skin framed by the black armor, some chanting, some wailing, others singing in a repetitive reel. Then under Siobhan's direction they approached William's black steel shell.

Piece by piece, they peeled away, searching for the man beneath until all at once the smoldering black steel revealed a chest wound so hideous, William's companions blanched. Withdrawing a round amulet of blue lapis from her pocket, Siobhan caressed William's face, and as she lay her head upon his heart, searching for the poison beneath, she saw the images of death and betrayal in Jerusalem.

She now saw the vision of William's grandfather Gerald, and the spell that had brought on the darkness, saw the serpent's glowing, diamond shaped eyes. Only now in his dream it was William trapped inside those eyes, trapped inside the wasteland of the light and the dark, in a war that raged inside himself.

Siobhan could see the wound where the diamond had lodged and how the poison had traveled to his grandfather Gerald's heart. It was a poison transferred to William and as she circled his blackened skin with the amulet, William's chest heaved like a volcano. Godobert and DeMonteforte recoiled as the blackness spewed from the wound and onto the floor, dripping from the table like thick, black pitch. But Siobhan continued and as the women wailed and moaned, she reached into the smoking hole and withdrew a black diamond splinter.

***

William's body was carried to a nearby home, to a bed stretched out before the fire. There, Godobert and DeMonteforte knelt before the lady Siobhan and kissed her hand. And by morning, when it was clear the worst had passed, the two knights begged her to care for the life of their friend.

"My lady," Godobert said as the sun came through the windows of the whitewashed cottage. "We must leave our friend William in your care."

"And what do you give in return?" Siobhan's mother demanded as she stepped in front of the young woman.

"Gold, of course," DeMonteforte said as he signaled Godobert to hand over his pouch. "Heal him well and upon his return I'll double it."

"Gold stolen from our saints and people will not have the power to heal," Siobhan said, as she gently signaled her mother to back away.

"Then what will?" DeMonteforte said, screwing up his nose in frustration.

"Honor our shrines and guard them as you would your own. Ask forgiveness and the saints will help me heal your friend."

The two mumbled to themselves as they mulled the terms of the deal, Godobert objecting most of all, but they soon saw the sense of it. And before the two departed, they assured the women the shrines to their Irish saints would no longer be molested.

***

That night Siobhan awoke beside William's bed as he slept a haunted sleep. Color was returning to his cheeks, but the war of the light and the dark still raged within and as she caressed his face and kissed his wound he drifted back into a gentle sleep.

Siobhan's eyes shone with compassion as she stared at the disarmed knight, lying helpless before her. Whoever he had been, whatever he had done before that night no longer mattered. He was the prophecy that fate had delivered into her arms. Dropping her nightshirt to the floor, she climbed into bed beside him and whispered a promise to St. Brigit that it would be a prophecy fulfilled.

***

Weeks went by and William grew healthier at the hands of the beautiful Siobhan. No longer was his skin a sullen grey, his eyes a pallid yellow. No longer did the nightmares of his grandfather's adventures haunt him in his dreams. For the first time in his life he was free to want his own dream and as the sweet Siobhan approached, he feigned a nightmare to draw her closer to his side. She was his dream now, his future in a new land with a new life and as she bent to caress his forehead he drew her towards him in a powerful embrace.

"I dreamed of you," he said, holding her with a strength that surprised her. "I dreamed you woke me from a sleep in a bright, frozen place. I dreamed that I touched you. And when I opened my eyes, you were here in this room."

Siobhan stared intensely as William struggled to remember.

"How can this be?" He said.

"Come," Siobhan said bruskly. "It's time you were up. The air is warm now and the sun will heal your wounds."

"Do you know what it means?" William demanded as Siobhan backed away and busied herself with his things.

"Yes," she said, turning toward him, cautiously. "Dress and come with me and I will show you what you dreamed."

Painfully William pulled himself from the bed and with Siobhan's help, managed to dress.

The air was warm and the meadows filled with flowers as they forded a wide river and climbed a steep hill. All seemed well until William noticed the beautiful Siobhan had fallen silent.

"The dream Siobhan. What did it mean?"

"It means that we are lovers, reunited from the long past and that past lives on in us today." A tear of happiness creased Siobhan's cheek as she slowed to dismount. "It's why you were delivered to me."

William seemed confused. "Then why do you cry?"

"This land and this river have great meaning to my people. It is said that it is where we first became. The river's name is Boinne. She carries the life force through our hearts. In that hill is the passage we traveled through on the rays of the sun to get here. There are many such passages. But that big one, Bru Oengusa is the most important. It is home to Angus, the son of our God of light. Come let me take you there."

Siobhan took William by the hand and lead him up the path to an egg shaped mound of earth covered by quartz crystals that glowed in the sun—surrounded by large, ornately carved oval curbstones.

"Legend says that our God built this home for himself but in the end was tricked into giving it to his son. In truth Angus is his father's younger-self and through some miracle both father and son are really one."

"That is the mystery of my faith as well," William said as he surveyed the strange but beautiful structure. "In separation from the father there is pain, but at the end of time when both are reunited there is joy in the sharing of a greater truth."

Siobhan ran her fingers around the shallow pockets dotting the curbstone at vital intervals in a strange pattern of diamonds and swirls. "It's been said that each of these pockets once held a jewel of different hue that lit the sky. But as the children dispersed across the seas, they each took with them a color from the rainbow until the sky turned black. I dreamed that you would bring us back the light."

William reached into his pouch and produced the stone. "We call this stone Abu for the ancient God that made the sun shine and the plants grow. From Sumer and Babylon to Jerusalem, the Jews kept it safe from harm, buried in their temple. I am told it is the key to the future but as yet I do not understand how. I ask you to share it with me that you may teach and I might learn."

Siobhan took the stone and fit it into a small circular hole at the center of a triple swirl near the entrance to the mound. Then smiling, pressed her body against it and closed her eyes. "Then we shall take it to where it will be safe until time ends and we shall call it castle Crom for our ancient God and Abu for yours. Castle Crom Abu, the castle where our dreams will grow."

Together, Siobhan and William traveled deeper into the countryside, to a place where Siobhan's family ruled as kings. And in a place known as Desmond they built their castle to Crom.

There, standing with Siobhan by the light of the full moon, William unstrapped the armor of the Black Knight and cast the cold lifeless shell to the bottom of the sacred lake, Gur. But as he stared into Siobhan's eyes, he knew that the war was far from over; that with or without him the war of the Light and the Dark would continue and that one day his children would be called upon to finish it. How they would respond to the calling he had no way of seeing, but as he stared into the shimmering pool, he prayed that the armor of the Black Knight would never be needed again.

GOING HOME

My desk light flickered and died as Big Ben struck five times. I cursed at the darkness until I looked out the window and saw that the whole town was dark.

It reminded me of that day at Transitron. I wondered whether it was somehow connected. London was an old city. Most of the oldest power stations were still on-line and as vulnerable to mechanical failure as terrorism. But there was something else about the frequent power outages that indicated the problem was bigger. Mainly, it was how the interference seemed to be getting into every kind of electrical device. Anything electronic, even portable electronic cameras and radios weren't immune and the interference was growing.

The government had been quick to allay fears as planes crashed, cities went dark and computers blinked on and off without explanation. But then the British govern ment was the most secretive Democracy in the Western World and where there was that amount of secrecy, there was plenty of room for doubt.

It all added to the general hysteria of crop circles, strange weather and UFO conspiracies that seemed to pop up everywhere and as I closed the book on Strongbow's Conquest, it all began to make sense. A pattern was forming, broad in scope and duration and as long as history itself.

Time was like some computer program that was coming to an end. Whether contained in the Mayan calender, Biblical scripture or

Sumerian texts, the cycle of human history known to the Hindus as the Kali Yuga was about to be completed and whether we liked it or not, the three dimensions of our world were about to be coalesced into a fourth.

Piecing together the general story from ancient myths and surviving documents, German, French and British nobles had become aware of the problem some nine hundred years ago. With the urging and assistance of small groups of exiled Jewish scholars, they had set out to find a way of preparing for it.

Reaching the holy land in the ninety-ninth year of the new millennium they began piecing the puzzle together bit by bit, but all the while, the truth of their mission and what lay ahead remained under their tight control.

Because of their privileged position, the original Crusaders were able to rapidly advance the course of European history and through their families and their knighthoods—maintain strict control of the secrets down through the centuries.

Held together by the power of the Pope in Rome, each knighthood was bound never to use the knowledge to gain advantage over the other, or more importantly to gain power over the Papacy itself. But as time went on they began to disagree and when the Pope crushed the Templar knights on November 22, 1307 for fear of their power and secret practices, a fierce struggle to control the remaining pieces of the puzzle ensued.

The French warred with the English, the English warred with the French and the Germans warred with themselves until war engulfed the entire continent. Whoever had secrets or was thought to posses them, whether heretic Christians, Cathars or mystical Jews, they were sought out, interrogated and destroyed.

But all the while, small bands of Norman mercenary knights escaped with pieces of the puzzle to Ireland and Scotland and after a few short years had managed to set themselves apart.

I withdrew the strange, glassy, high tech marble from my pocket that I'd picked up at Transitron, the day I'd knocked the Dream

Catcher to the floor. No bigger than an eyeball and nothing special to look at, it reminded me of an aggie I'd played with as a kid. But inside the glass crystal lay a sheer film of high tech electronics that invested the bearer with the powers of creation through light. Was this a new idea? With all the talk about the Grail and attaining it through so called philosopher's stones, I began to wonder if Rick's Dream Catcher technology wasn't new at all, but very, very old. Maybe the whole idea of creation through light was so old it had been at the center of Gilbert De Clare's quest for most of a millennium.

And if it was, then there might still be a real Grail out there just waiting to be uncovered, a real Grail just waiting for the right person to come along. As I penciled a quick note to Alissa, I knew she would understand. She'd followed my journey for as long as I could remember and if anyone was prepared for what I was about to step into, it was her.

I sensed that we were all on the verge of some new experience. And though I feared for what that experience might mean for my daughter, I feared more for the world as it was. Whatever this Grail was, it had to lead to a better place and now I had a good idea where to find it.

***

Alissa awoke later that morning and noted the clock had stopped; not an unusual occurrence but today it felt different, almost as if not just the clock, but time itself had stopped.

"Dad!" She said as she walked into the front hall. "The power's off again."

It was a moment before she spotted the note, written in that distinctive parochial school scrawl, picked it up and read it out loud.

Dear Alissa,

I'm off. Not a dream this time. It's
real. Will call in a couple of days
Be back by Christmas.
Love Dad.

Alissa finished the note, just the doorbell buzzed loudly, signaling the power had suddenly surged back on.

"Just a minute," she said thinking the buzzer had stuck only to be surprised at the sight of Rick Kendall standing at the door.

"Oh!" she said, startled. "I thought you might be my father."

"He's not here?" Rick asked, seemingly alarmed at the prospect he'd lost track of Paul again. "When will he be back?"

"For you? Probably never, " Alissa replied, smiling.

Rick seemed nervous. "That's not helpful."

"I tried. I really did," Alissa said, leaning against the doorpost. "I did want to thank you for helping me find him but he'd just as soon see you burned at the stake as get his book."

"Then just tell me where I should set myself on fire so he doesn't miss it."

Rick's idea was on target and Alissa laughed.

"The boss is really bearing down on you isn't he?"

"An hour of your time, just an hour is all I need. Then you can explain it to him."

"An hour?" Alissa said staring at the clock, still stuck at 5:55. "All right. But no guarantees."

***

"I understand why your father hates me so. A lot of people do, I'm sure," Rick said as they walked through Russell square and entered a trendy looking cyber cafe. "But as a news professional, there are decisions that have to be made . . . . "

"That's the point," Alissa said as they found a table with an online computer.

"Rick. Call me Rick."

"O.K. Rick. You see, my father thinks, as the public's voice you have a responsibility. He's kind of from the old school, I mean the very old school where the bard maintained the balance between heaven and earth for his culture? It's a simple philosophy. You do understand philosophy," she said condescendingly.

"Yes. But what has that got to do with my business?" Rick said impatiently.

"Everything. You guys don't just keep the truth from people, you keep it from each other, even yourselves. Yet you so believe what you say is the truth you don't even know what's true or false anymore. I mean he thinks its really bad and I agree. Just look around you. Look at all the cars, the noise, the pollution, the congestion. Are they a good thing? No. Is there a better solution? Yes. Do we get one? No. Why? Because the carpark man has a friend in Parliament, the minister for transport has a million shares of Ford Motor Company in his portfolio and the asphalt industry conglomerate owns a half dozen newspapers. The real question of cars is never even addressed and it never will be."

"So what's that got to do with philosophy?" Rick asked.

"It's all wrong." Alissa said, glaring at Rick. "We're out of balance with nature and out of harmony with heaven and it just can't be. If people don't know what's going on they can't make the necessary changes and if we can't change we die. The farmer, the cab driver, the cook who makes your eggs can't be kept in the dark just so a handful of people can keep having it the way they like. Sooner or later things break down or blow up."

Rick smiled wanly as Alissa nodded toward a punk rocker at a nearby table wearing a perfect purple Mohawk. "And the only way people know what to do is to let them in on what you know. No secrecy."

"It's a complicated issue," Rick said, scrunching up his forehead as if truly confounded.

"No. It's very simple." Alissa said. "I'm not talking about what the government wants you to believe so you won't question their authority, or Wall Street wants you to believe so you'll run out and buy the newest, fastest whatever. I'm talking about *the truth,* that thing that helps you get through the day, the thing that gives your life meaning."

"We live in a complex world where there is no single truth." Rick said, struggling to make points.

"Let's not pad the delusion Rick." Alissa said, shaking her head in frustration. "You guys lie about everything. I know you lie and what you don't lie about you leave out."

Rick sat back, surprised by the sudden left hook Alissa had thrown. "So what do you want me to do?"

"Publish my father's book."

Rick sighed deeply. "But that's what I always intended . . .

"Just the way he wrote it."

"You really hate me, don't you? I mean for what you think I did to your mother."

"My mother had great hopes for you, Rick." Alissa said, getting up to leave. "The last thing she said to me before she got on that plane for Afghanistan was: 'This guy is tough and smart, just like your father. He'll get the story right.' Well Rick, you never told that story. You never even bothered to revise it or reform it or punch it up. You just dropped it like a hot potato. For me that's truth. The truth from my mother who meant everything to me. You insult her by proving her wrong."

Rick's face turned white as Alissa turned on her heel and walked out. As much as he wanted that book, she had struck at something inside. She had mocked him not just for what he did, she had mocked him for what he was—and as the hollow sounding cyber voice intoned its message, a voice inside told him that she was right.

"Want to make that big deal in the new millennium? Do it on the Internet."

REVELATION, THE BOOK OF

After a brisk walk to Victoria station through the fog shrouded London morning I found myself in the compartment of a westbound train comparing a Foders map of Ireland to those of Strongbow's Conquest. Amazingly enough the two were strongly similar, the cart tracks and scattered villages of 1170 still providing the basic blueprint for the roads and towns of the next millennium.

It was impossible to fully comprehend the brutality of medieval warfare, how these men had hacked and hued their way through the countryside, personally murdering by hand, hundreds, perhaps thousands of people. Far easier to imagine modern warfare with its impersonal, detached killing than to imagine the thought of a man in chain mail and leather, jamming a sharp sword into some poor peasant's chest who'd been unlucky enough to be standing in his way.

The whole idea put modern life and our distance from it into perspective and if anything, that distance separated us from who we really were. What modern soldier with his kevlar, zip gun and tactical air support would bear up psychologically under the daily slaughter of medieval warfare, where you looked each man you killed in the eye and smelled his fear before you gutted him? I doubted many. Warfare back then was a calling, a priesthood of death where the basic rules of life were clear as black and white. It was men's bargain with the devil.

What women gave, men took away, and what they took, they took very seriously. After my visits with the Black Knight the idea put me in a strange mood. In a way I almost believed he had come to take me. Reaching out to me over nearly a thousand years.

"May I?" A soft, female voice asked, snapping me from my daydream. For a moment I thought she was a vision, long, attractive with fine reddish brown hair. But as she stretched to secure her overnight bag with delicate graceful hands—her slit skirt revealing just a hint of a graceful, exquisitely formed thigh—I realized she was much, much more.

She smiled as I nodded and she assumed the empty seat across the aisle, removing her large round sun glasses to reveal penetrating violet eyes.

"Traveling to Ireland?" She asked in a tone that suggested more than just a casual interest.

I nodded again, still too deep in thought and too taken by her vision to risk a garbled answer. But she persisted.

"Beautiful country. Misty, magical even. Searching for lost ancestors?"

"I've tried," I finally answered, clearing my throat. "But there seems to be large gaps in the records."

"It's easier to assume someone's property if they never had a record of owning it," she said with an unusual cynicism. "So you're Catholic?"

"Originally. It's hard not to be as a Fitzgerald."

The woman seemed taken aback by the name, letting out a sigh and dropping her eyes. "It's no wonder there's no trace. Your family's been a thorn in the Royal backside since day two. But then it wasn't entirely England's fault. There were others who wanted the ancient practices extinguished as well."

"Ancient practices?" I asked, now drawn like a magnet to the woman's serene face.

"Divination, prophecy, geomancy, necromancy—ways of linking the present with the past." She stopped, reaching a long, thin hand across the aisle. "Forgive me. I'm Jill Westcock."

"Paul," I replied, returning the gesture. "And how would you know so much about that?"

The woman smiled. "I'm a witch."

I resisted a laugh, but couldn't conceal the grin.

"I know. You don't think I look the type," she said reassuringly. "Neither did I before the crossover."

"Crossover?"

Jill spoke in a whisper, careful to avoid waking the young passenger, dozing by the window. "It was like waking up in another world except more real, much more real than this one. In fact it was so real I had no idea I was actually asleep to this world.

"You were dreaming!" I said, the woman's experience mirroring mine. "So how did you get back?"

Jill's eyes sparkled as her red lips drew back in a broad smile.

"A Catholic priest was called to perform last rights thinking I was dead. Something he said, something in the sacrament of Extreme Unction pulled me back. But ever since, the door's been open."

"And where does it go?" I asked.

"Anywhere you want it to," the woman said slowly and seductively. "Since the millennium, the possibilities are endless."

"Since the millennium." I knew what she meant. Up to and through the millennium my dreams had been getting more and more powerful. But now, like hers, they had become separate realities like stations on this train line, where I could come and go at will, visit and remember what I'd done there. But one look at the countryside, out at the ravages of the old industrial cities lining the tracks, reminded me of how brutal the trip had been. "It does seem we've used this place up, doesn't it?" I said.

"What you see are only the echoes of what once was real," the long legged beauty with the delicate hands responded wistfully as she settled herself into the chair with a self-confidence I found appealing. "It's already over."

"So this isn't real?" I asked watching two young children run past the open car door, playing tag in the train corridor.

Jill suddenly bent low again, a watchful eye on the sleeping student. "Nuclear bombs, biological warfare, UFO's and crop circles? The egg's been cracked a long time deary. Of course, things still look the same, but the illusion won't remain that way for long. The end of time is coming and no one can stop the clock."

The conductor maneuvered past the children and entered, tipping his hat to Jill and waking the student as he gathered tickets.

"Bristol in two hours madam," he said, smiling weakly through bad teeth, turned brown by years of tobacco.

"So where do we go?" I asked, as the conductor stared at us suspiciously, punched his ticket and turned to leave.

Jill waited until the man had left, then slowly slid her hand across the aisle until it rested on my knee. "I thought that might be something you could tell me."

***

Alissa returned home and climbed the one flight to the apartment. As she approached she noticed something was wrong. She had been surprised by Rick's visit but she knew she'd locked the door and now that door was open. As she entered, she recoiled at the broken lock and overturned furniture. The apartment had been ransacked—no—examined was a better word, inside and out. Her favorite chair was sliced neatly as were the couch cushions and seat backs, the stuffing extracted and placed on the floor. Someone had come looking for something they wanted very badly. And as she backed away and ran for help, she realized her father's deepest fears for his unpublished manuscript were coming true.

***

Rick's phone rang as he sat in his office before his screens, nursing a killer headache. Lord Gilbert's voice was still ringing in his ears and the impact was still settling in. For months he'd been having strange nightmares about Lord Gilbert, finding himself in conversations with the man that seemed personal and at times uncomfortable, but he'd ignored them. Now he was beginning to wonder whether the dreams had been dreams at all and what he was about to hear would not quiet an already unsettled mood.

"Kendall." He said lifting the receiver.

It was Alissa.

"Just an hour, you said!" She screamed into the phone from the ruins of her apartment as a police detective wrote up the damage.

"Who is this?" Rick said, holding the phone away from his ear for fear the shouts would further damage his already throbbing brain.

"Alissa Fitzgerald, that's who! Who else's apartment have you ravaged today? My father said you were trouble, but I had no idea how far you'd go."

Concerned, Rick looked around nervously. "Look. I can't talk here. Let me meet you."

"Oh no! Haven't you caused enough insult already?"

"Yes. Probably," Rick said, trying to be thoughtful. "But I've got to know more about this book thing of your father's."

"I don't have time."

Now it was Rick screaming into the phone: "Then I'll help!"

"No way."

"Alissa, it's important," Rick said, pleading. "I mean it's really important. Your father's life may be in danger."

Alissa didn't know what it was. Perhaps it was her mother's broken picture staring up at her from the floor. But there must have been something, perhaps the tone in Rick's voice that finally convinced her.

"All right. Meet me at the front gate of the Museum in two hours. But don't be surprised if I change my mind."

Rick hung up and stared at the monitors filled with scenes of disasters and riots, plagues and atrocities. Ever since he'd come to work at Transitron he'd had the notion that Lord Gilbert's interest in Paul's book was unusual, but he'd brushed it off. Now, since the board meeting it was beginning to make sense and Alissa's call had set his mind to racing. It was getting harder to think of things the way he used to and it wasn't just the constant violence of the TV screens. His usually rock solid view of the world and his place in it was shaking, and it bothered him.

His time at Transitron had taught him many things. He acknowledged Paul's complaint; that Afghanistan had been the center of a massive shift in America's ethos. The election of an actor as President in 1980 had obscured the lines between image and reality and that distinction had never recovered. Now he was suffering from that queezy feel that nothing was as it seemed, that life had become some swirling electronic mirage and he was caught in it. As he reached for his coat and rushed from the building, away from the high powered antennas that beamed and received signals from all over the globe, he fought the sense of panic that was beginning to overcome him.

***

He was right to be concerned. Lord Gilbert had hired Rick because of his previous relationship to Paul, thinking it would move things along. Instead, it had only made the situation stickier at a time when he needed results. So, as Rick left the building and headed for the British Museum he reached for the phone with the intention of throwing the whole business into a higher gear.

"Get me the Home Secretary."

***

Sirens screamed through the thick smoke as Rick stood outside the museum's main gate unaware that Alissa had snuck up from behind. "More of your handiwork?" She said, as she seemed to materialize out of the darkness.

"IRA," Rick sniffed, covering his face with a handkerchief to keep out the smoke.

"They've vowed to finish off The City. It's some kind of symbol for them and they won't stop until it's destroyed."

"Well, it was prophesied by no less than four Irish Saints," Alissa said, smugly. "This war will last until the day of judgement."

"And I suppose God's going to turn all this over to a bunch of terrorists?"

"Do you always talk in sound bites?" She said motioning him toward the doors and away from the smoke. "It's not about terrorism."

"Then educate me," Rick said, his head still throbbing from the smoke and the day's constant assault.

"You really don't see any of it do you? With all your security and surveillance, with your satellites and snooping cameras you haven't got a clue."

"And you know?"

"Maybe my father does," Alissa said, stopping Rick coldly just inside the doors. "And maybe you sent someone to steal his manuscript to find out?"

"I didn't send anybody."

"Then who did? Who knew I'd be out at the cyber cafe with you during that time?"

"I don't know," Rick said, staring off into the distance.

In his heart he knew well of Gilbert's weird desire for Paul's book. But he couldn't reveal his suspicions just yet. He needed more facts and more time to process what was beginning to seem impossible to believe. So he held back.

"But if I knew more. Maybe I could figure that out," he said.

Alissa was suspicious and her look said so but she let it go, for the moment.

"All right. But there's something in there I want to see."

Inside, Alissa led Rick through the galleries of the museum, through the long ages of Britain.

"Did your father's move here have something to do with this dreaming business?" Rick asked as they moved toward an exhibit of ancient Celtic culture.

"He called this an outpost of the dream," she said as they passed Knights on horseback staring out at them from an exhibit on the Middle Ages. "There's a magic here. You can feel it." Alissa pointed as they passed a model of Stonehenge. "The holy Grail, Druids and crop circles, dungeons and dragons? Only here it wasn't a game. It was real and people believed it was real."

"But it's a myth." Rick protested.

"It is!" Alissa said. "But what is myth?"

"A fiction, fantasy. Something made up."

Alissa slowed as they approached the end of a long line leading to a roped off section of the museum, labeled in large swirling letters, Celtic life in early Britain. She smiled snidely. "That definition could just as easily describe the evening news, couldn't it?"

Rick was caught by surprise. "You sound like your father."

"I'll give you the benefit of the doubt. Every age interprets their own time, in their own way, in their own language. Just because you don't happen to see the past with the same eyes doesn't make it a fantasy. Most cultures share the same mythology, they just put different spins on it. What you have to do is get down to the real message and that's where the myth can be revealing."

The couple turned the corner Alissa had visited with her father just a day ago and shrieked. "It's gone. He was right here. The face was the same, the eyes and everything." She started to tremble. "Kendall, be honest with me. What's going on here?"

Rick snapped back defensively. "You think I made this disappear?"

"What is it you want to know? What is it you think is so damned important that you have to keep everybody else from knowing?"

Kendall scratched his head. "I don't know Alissa, really. Not unless it's that number thing."

"What number thing?"

"That number your father said kept turning up all over the place. #117. The room number where the American Ambassador to Afghanistan was killed."

"I know all about that. It seemed to signify something, like the beginning of a chain of events. If that man hadn't been killed, the Russians wouldn't have invaded. If the Russians didn't invade, Pakistan wouldn't have needed to develop the bomb. If Pakistan didn't have the bomb India wouldn't have gone to red alert and a whole lot of people would sleep a lot better."

Rick seemed grimmer than usual. "It's not about Pakistan and India. I'm afraid it's too late for that. It's about time."

Alissa was surprised. "Time? Just time?"

"To be more specific. The end of time. I thought it was crazy too at first. I mean it's not exactly something you think about. Then it started showing up in the electronics. Just little glitches at first, barely noticeable. Programs weren't running when they should. Because we're on a world-wide schedule we have to synchronize with the earth's geomagnetic field. We have to factor in sun spots. No matter what we did we couldn't keep in sync. Then it started to break up. Parts of the web just disappeared, then reappeared at recurring intervals: But only at the intervals between 1 and 17."

"Like a code?"

Rick's eyes searched for clues. "A code we don't know the meaning of. I've got to find your father to help me figure it out. Do you know where he is?"

"Wales, Ireland. I don't know. He's probably following the book, the one he got at that little shop you traced him to."

"Well, we found him there once. Maybe we'll find him there again." Rick said.

SIMON AND THE ORACLE

As the train lurched through the little Welsh towns, all I could think of, was what the woman Jill had said. "The end of this space is coming and no one can stop it." Were we really only echoes of what was—living in a reality that was growing thinner as the end of time approached? It was nearly impossible to imagine, but the idea seemed to fit the situation and the feeling I was under. The fabric of time did seem thinner, once meaningful events, institutions and nations, even sexes seemed to be blending together into a blur. Nothing was the same any longer, not even the weather.

My dreams seemed to be answering this confusion by tying the past into the present and as time raced ahead I tried to fit them all together.

But how did it all work? What was this thing that I was doing and were other people doing it too? They had to be, even if they didn't know it. Perhaps in their dreams everyone was weaving their own pasts into the present too, all to be joined together some morning when they woke up and found a new reality.

But what would that reality look like? The whole business was getting weirder by the day, the pattern of my life fitting the mythology of the Grail quest so closely, as if I was playing into a role without even trying.

I was living the mystical experience—chugging through towns and villages recorded in Grail legends of a thousand years ago and the closer I came to my destination the more I became my dreams. What those dreams would bring next I couldn't imagine, but I sensed the answer was to be found in the mists of Ireland—in the buried remains of the past.

"I couldn't help overhearing your conversation with the lady." The man in the dark round glasses seated by the window asked. The young ministerial student in his tired black clothes and worn shoes had been biding his time and now that the long legged Jill had just slipped off to the powder room, he saw his chance. "My name is Simon, Simon Templar. As a student of the ministry I find it all quite interesting."

"Do you believe that time is coming to an end?" I replied, thinking how oddly studious the young man appeared.

"It's been foretold. The ancient world was obsessed with it. Stonehenge, the Maya temples ... "

"I thought all that was built for the farmers to keep track of the seasons."

"One doesn't plant corn with a calender that measures thousands of years. One keeps track of something else. And I for one think that something else is about to happen again."

Simon glanced but barely acknowledged Jill as she returned to her seat.

"And what do you think that is?" I asked.

Simon scrunched down, eyeing Jill suspiciously. "All the ancient scriptures refer to the End Time. The bible talks about it. Plato referred to it in the Timaeus. Time begins, time ends and then starts over again in another form."

Barely able to contain herself, Jill chimed in. "And then what? We all ascend to heaven?"

Simon was brief. "If that's where you want to go."

"What church did you study the ministry for?" I asked.

"Church of England, of course. But the theology is all basically the same. Either you believe it or you don't. Like your lady here said. It all gets somewhat controver sial when you get down to the heart of it and start looking at what it really means. The Irish monks knew what it was all about. Just like those native women in South America. Irish monks were free to travel all over the world and they weren't afraid of the truth."

The idea surprised me. "So what kind of Christianity did they practice?"

"Nothing like what you'd think of as Christian today. Their writings are really quite strange—bizarre rituals for communicating with spirits and demons, raising the dead, walking between the worlds," he said, raising an eyebrow. "There are some distinct strains of belief that predate even Judaism."

"Is that possible?" I asked, finding the logic more than hard to follow. "You're saying there are strains of Christianity in Ireland that not only predate Rome, but Judaism as well?"

"I'm saying there are strains of an ancient pre-Celtic metaphysics that spanned Europe, the Near East and the Middle East in the fourth millennium B.C. that evidenced itself in all the religions of the world and eventually manifest themselves in Babylon, Judea and in early Christianity. It was only natural that Irish monks should return those strains to Ireland as Christianity, simply because that's where they'd originated."

"I've never heard this." I offered, thinking of the consequences.

"You're not supposed to. But the idea that most of us were brought up with—that Moses descended from the mount with a copy of the King James version of the bible, in English, is what a Buddhist would call a sublime illusion, if you get my meaning? All religion is a vast syncretion of ideas and beliefs accrued over a long period of time, but only by getting back to the original idea can we ever hope to make sense out of it."

"So what have you made out of it?" I asked.

Simon wiped the steam from the window and looked out at the growing darkness.

"I had a theory at school, a crazy idea, but then I was a student," he said quietly, "that as light is composed of all the colors of the spectrum, we are composed of light. In essence we are all beings of light and through some celestial transmission process interacting with dark matter, life formed on earth. It seemed extreme even to me at the time but the more I studied the mythology and ancient texts the more I came to see "the light" as some kind of technical metaphor. With the inventions of the last few years, laser discs and fiber optics, it doesn't seem strange to me any more. Any message can be carried through light and the faster we advance the technology the closer we get ... "

"To creation?" Jill said as she stood in the compartment door, bearing down on Simon with an annoyed glare. "Please don't stop on my account. It all sounds very interesting."

Simon paused for a moment, distracted as Jill took her seat, then began again as if nothing had occurred.

"Are you familiar with the concept of the Monad or Monas?" He asked, as he scrunched his nose up underneath horn rimmed glasses. "It's the foundation of Monasticism. The study of the Monad."

"Actually, Yes." I admitted. "I once dreamed about the subject and looked it up."

"Then you may know it all has to do with optics. There is a Monad of form and a Monad of spirit. Think of the Monad of spirit as God's idea, traveling through space looking for a shape in which to fit and the Monad of form is that shape."

"But how does he get that shape?" I asked, watching Jill's growing impatience with the nerdish Simon.

"That's where we come in, isn't it," she said, pursing her lips into a smile.

Simon looked toward her, confused as if he'd never seen a woman before, then returned to his conversation. "We're just beginning to understand how matter translates information from light at different wave lengths. Light makes things grow, mutate—but if you split the light even further with a prism let's say using a diamond or some other crystal you could easily break the light off into sub-frequencies creating vast patterns, maybe even universes."

"But all of that is still without substance," I said, thinking back to my experience at Transitron and the Dream Catcher technology. "I can accept that God, whoever he is, sent the design for my hand here to earth through light. But my hand is made of matter."

Simon seemed to grow turned on by the challenge. "Three hundred years ago Swedenborg theorized that the universe was constantly in a state of creation maintained by two wavelike flows, one directly from God, the other from God through matter, to us. According to Oxford scholar Dr. George Dole, that makes our world and everything in it like an electronic interference pattern between matter and spirit, positioned exactly where the waves meet. Swedenborg didn't have the words three-hundred years ago. But today we'd call that point of becoming, a hologram. This whole bloody existence is a hologram from beginning to end. God's creation through light."

Jill Westcock said nothing as I sat back and considered the idea.

"It explains everything. All the ancient texts viewed from this perspective from the Persian Sufis to the bible, make perfect sense." Simon said, now urgent to convince me.

"And where does it lead you, Jerusalem, the pyramids?"

"No." He said in a whisper. "Ireland."

***

Mary Underhill led Rick and Alissa down the narrow aisle of the old Soho shop and into the back room where the table was set for visitors.

"Were you expecting someone?" Rick asked, staring at the fresh cut flowers and ornate Victorian tea service.

"Yes," Mary answered, smiling at Alissa as she poured tea into the waiting cups. "I used to entertain quite a bit in the afternoon, but then Lord Abercrombie was poisoned and the business just slacked off."

Rick returned his cup to the saucer, causing a wry smile to break out on Mary's lips.

"Some people take this business very seriously, people in high places. I hope a young man like yourself can learn there are many things you might not understand."

Embarrassed, Rick politely tasted the tea and smiled. "It's very good."

"We've come about my father, Mary." Alissa said. "He's disappeared again and we'd hoped you could help figure out what's going on."

"I suppose I could gaze into my crystal," she said, motioning toward the fist size piece of quartz sitting in the middle of the table. "But I don't think in your father's case, it's necessary."

Alissa bit her lip as she stared at Rick.

"Your father is completing a journey his soul began a very long time ago. It's only a question of locating him in the final chapter."

Rick squirmed, startled by Mary's frankness.

"That's why you gave my father the book," Alissa said. *"Strongbow's Conquest."*

"Yes. His experience at the Templar Church seemed to have jogged his memory. I just hope its all remembered in time before the Great Cycle is completed."

Rick shifted in his seat, trying to ease his discomfort with Mary's message by making light of it. "You sound as if you believe the end of the world was imminent."

Mary responded with pity. "My dear boy. When the Bee Gees went disco, it was obvious the end of this world was imminent. It's only a question of what's next that I'm concerned with—whether we go on from here or go back to the beginning."

"Mary, please." Alissa said, stopping Rick as he tried to rebut. "There isn't much time."

Mary cast a stony gaze at Rick. "Yes, time. That and the number 117. Isn't that what you said?"

"The number 117 is more than a sacred number. As you've already discovered, the number itself disguises a number system between 1 and 17. The disguise protects it from being used by the uninitiated."

"How do you mean "used?" Alissa asked.

Mary continued. "Invoked magically to gain power in a cosmic sense. Chanted as an incantation by someone who's studied the holy texts that unravel the mysteries of the universe. Even though the number has no obvious value it corresponds to a value in the great scheme of things—like a combination lock. That's why anniversaries are so important—why prayers are repeated over and over. Sacred numbers are an address for opening up to higher powers."

Rick tried to show he understood. "You mean the way a computer program needs repetitive code to run a program."

"Oh, very good Mr. Kendall. We shall send you to the head of the class." She said mockingly, as she rolled her eyes.

"Your father's family sailed to Ireland on its power in 117-0, or in fact they may have been drawn by it, assuming they already knew the power of the number, which is what I assume."

Alissa tried to follow. "Power?"

"The most powerful number in creation. Actually it IS the number of creation. That's why Henry II ran over there to claim Ireland for himself. But it was already too late. The Geraldine priests cracked the real Bible Code within 70 years of the first Crusade and brought it with them to Ireland."

"So what exactly is the secret of the number?" Alissa asked.

Rick sat on his hands like a schoolboy, trying to remain calm. "Your friend here seems to like computers. Do the math. 1+2+3 . . .

"Equals one hundred and fifty three." Rick said.

"And what is that?" Mary said instructively.

Rick became increasingly uncomfortable, shifting in his seat under Mary's scrutiny. "Your serious about this, right?"

"And so had you better be, dear boy."

Alissa grew upset. "Mary please. Get on with it."

"It is the mathematical representation of the Hieros Gamos, the sacred marriage between heaven and earth." She said smiling. "That marriage is represented by the blood red X—the vesica piscis to be exact anatomically."

Rick and Alissa stared blankly but spoke simultaneously. "Anatomically?"

"The entry to the Holy of Holies, the Tabernacle, the matrix. Didn't you take sex education as a boy? The Irish Christians used to have carvings of women over the doors to their churches, legs spread wide in welcome. It was a welcome that Gilbert De Clare's son Richard had every intention of accepting 800 years ago. By sending out the numerical symbol of that message into the universe, the universe responds accordingly. My dear man, what you and your technical whiz-kids have been courting with your electronic signal is beyond imagining."

Rick sat, awed. "My God. I didn't know."

"Your Lord Gilbert knew then and your Lord Gilbert knows now. I assume with all likelihood that he is the very same person who dabbled in alchemy and is now about to give the new electronic world a life of its own." Mary said.

Rick held his head in both hands. "Shit. No wonder the electronics have been breaking up. We've been courting it."

"Then you'd better listen and listen good, so you'll know what your in for." Mary said, chastising Rick. "These people have been at it for a long time my boy. Learn from what they did and maybe you can figure out how to help. Otherwise get out of the way."

Mary began where *Strongbow's Conquest* left off.

"Merlin had prophesied the conquest of Ireland," Mary said as the room seemed to darken around them. "And Nest knew her children would someday create a kingdom that would never be destroyed. But the actual invasion was done on behalf of Strongbow. And when it became obvious that Maurice and William and FitzStephen had fulfilled the prophecy, he soon made his way to collect on it."

Waving here hands and whispering low, Mary seemed to pull the images from the air and as Rick and Alissa listened, they were soon drawn into the world that Paul had been living in his dreams.

IRELAND 1170 DIVINE VENGEANCE

The earl was of high descent, for he was born of the noble stock of the house of Clare. Yet withal, so far, a man whose family was better than his fortune; who had more blue blood than brains, and whose pedigree was longer than his purse. He was called Strongbow, apparently by the Flemings and the English in his service in S. Wales, a nickname borne first by his father Gilbert. He succeeded to his earldom in 1149, but was in disgrace with the king, who had deprived him of his estate.

Giraldus Cambrensis

Strongbow was deliriously happy as his warship approached the coast. Years of warfare and bad luck added to the high cost of making a pure Philosopher's stone had lost him most of his father's estates in Wales and Normandy. But Ireland would change all that. An entire island, the first and last preserve of the most ancient mysteries, mysteries King Henry II had turned most of France and England upside down for, were now laid at his feet thanks to an army of Grail knights known as the Geraldines.

As he waded through the surf, his long red hair flowing down his shoulders, he smiled without a care. Of all the Crusaders, Gilbert's son had finally achieved the kingdom he had sought with his Philosopher's stone, the Grail kingdom. And now as his long arms dangled in the surf, he had come to claim it.

There was a power here, the raw power of the four elements kept preserved through the long years of Roman Empire and Dark Ages, the Vikings and the Norman conquest.

Here, far from the probing eye of the Holy See, the Irish scholars had been free to delve into the secrets of the past and had kept an ancient door open to a world beyond time, a world Strongbow believed he would now have all to himself.

"My father had dreamed it would be like this. From that very first day on his voyage to Jerusalem he knew the Grail—so long vanished from this world—would someday be restored. And now I, his son, Lord Richard De Clare, Earl of Pembroke do hereby claim that dream to be real."

Standing with his brothers and cousins on the beach, William greeted his Lord as he arrived, but he knew it would not be as easy for Strongbow as he'd thought. Strongbow knew the cost of secret knowledge, but William understood it. After a year in this strange land he also understood the road to the Grail required Brigit's approval and that was a burning test that lay just ahead.

***

Torches burned late that night in Strongbow's camp as the battle scarred veterans of the Geraldine invasion shared stories with the new arrivals. With advanced skills and Norman armor, those first battles had been easily won. But there was more on Strongbow's mind that first night than strategy and tactics and as the revelries continued he slipped off into the night for a glimpse of the Grail.

William prayed calmly as Strongbow quietly entered the small chapel behind him, the fiery apparition of Brigit hovering over the glowing red stone on the altar.

"It's true what I've been told." Strongbow said breathlessly. "My eyes have never seen such beauty or such terror." Awed by the sight, he stumbled forward a few short steps—nearly tripping over William. "And now it belongs to me."

"No Strongbow. You must not." William said as he blocked Strongbow's effort to seize the stone. "You will be consumed."

"I am the master of the fire now. I am the rightful owner of the Grail of being, the Lord of Ireland—fulfillment of the prophecy. This was taken for my father and rightfully belongs to me."

"It was taken to fulfill the contract of the Red King and made sacred with his blood. Are you prepared to sacrifice yours?" William struggled to hold Strongbow back, but he was weakened under the power of the large Earl with his long arms and huge strength.

"I possess my own martyrs blood, fresh from the killing at Solstice Night." Strongbow said, dangling a bloody scarf up to the fire's light. Here, see the blood from the archbishop Becket, the holy victim who consecrates our invasion? Or perhaps you would like for your blood to be spilled instead."

Strongbow clubbed William with the butt handle of his heavy sword, then used his enormous strength to send him sprawling down the aisle of the small chapel, before reaching out for the stone.

"No. Don't!" William screamed one more time. But it was too late. Filled with his own sense of power, Strongbow lifted the glowing red stone from beneath the shimmering image of Brigit and raised it to his eyes.

"It is incredible. The power it bestows. I see everything. I hear everyone." He said, as Brigit bent low over him.

"Don't you love me the best?" She said, a fiery smile on her face.

"Oh, I do. I really, really do love you the best."

"Then come with me and be my love."

In an instant, Brigit encircled Strongbow, the red stone clutched tightly to his chest. Spinning a beautiful web of fire he was soon engulfed, flames pouring into his open mouth. But as Brigit filled him,

Strongbow's delight turned to terror. No longer the bragging conqueror, he threw himself to the floor and begged for help. "William. I need you. Stop her before she kills me."

Shielding his eyes from the intense flame, William crawled toward the altar, hand outstretched for the stone. And as Strongbow released his grip, the fire subsided. Writhing in what appeared to be agony, Strongbow rose from the floor. But miraculously, he seemed untouched by the flame. Yet in his eyes the flame still burned and as he struggled to the door, it was obvious that more than just his pride had been burned away.

It wasn't long before Brigit's tests began for Strongbow as they had for William and all the others, calling to him as visions, then haunting him in his dreams. And though he won his battles by day, driving the Irish from their homes and tearing down their shrines, Strongbow was beset by losses at night, hounded by Brigit, the spirit of fire who tested him as he slept.

"Come to me Strongbow? Don't you love me the best," she said as she licked at his flesh and burned in his heart, just the way she'd burned the Black Knight.

Strongbow wanted the lady of fire. He wanted her power just as the others had, but the man-made magic of his Philosopher's stone proved no use and like the archers that day at her chapel, he withered under her scorching caress. His Catholic priests and clerics stood by helplessly as he wrestled on his deathbed.

"It's her. It's her that's killing me!" He screamed, as they watched his skin turn black, but there was nothing to be done as Brigit, the fiery dart burned the flesh from his bones.

Strongbow was dead and so was his father Gilbert's dream. Upon seeing the success of the invasion Henry II quarantined the country then sailed immediately to Dublin to claim it, declaring the Geraldines enemies of the realm.

But by then they were far beyond his reach. Far away, in the ancient Kingdom of Desmond, a castle named Crom was raised near the sacred lake Gur. And there, in the chapel before a Geraldine priest,

William joined his family to Siobhan's and thereby to the children of the Tuatha De Danaan.

Alissa took a deep breath as Mary reached for the delicate China pot and poured another cup of tea. "And that's where it ends?" Alissa asked sadly.

"It's where the book ends," Mary answered, her tone now more serious than before.

"But it was just the preparation for Act IV."

Mary folded her hands across her lap and lowered her head, dropping into a trance, then in a slow rhythmic chant picked up the story:

"For the next four centuries William's family grew. And just as the prophecy had predicted, they prospered. Embracing the Irish and their ancient practices they became so powerful the English Kings were soon left with little more to govern than the slums of Dublin.

In 1307 the power of the Knights Templar was destroyed by Papal decree leaving the Geraldines unchallenged for possession of the stone. Unable to complete their conquest, the English Kings grew embittered.

With their successful merging of Norman and Celt, the Geraldines had become the Grail's protectors and as they attained more and more of the mysterious powers of the Tuatha De Danaan, so did their ability to use it.

The Desmond Earls soon surpassed the magical powers of the Knights Templar. Legends claimed their marriage to the old Celtic ways enabled them to pass between the worlds, some say even mixing with the magical people. But their growing power provoked terrible jealousies even within the family and in the year 1560 it exploded.

One painful jealousy that would prove crucial, pitted the fourteenth Earl, Gerald FitzGerald against his own step-son Black Tom Butler and as the two ragtag armies of farmers and peasants lined up across from one another in a Desmond meadow, they threatened to drag the entire family into war.

Something had gone wrong. Somehow in attempting to keep the family bound together in kinship, Joan Butler had angered her son

Tom by marrying Gerald after his father's death, and as she rode frantically back and forth between them, she prayed she could make peace.

For two weeks she negotiated between the warring camps as their servants and tenants waited in the rain with pitchforks to tear each other apart. And in the end she succeeded.

But as Gerald rode from the field of battle with the woman he loved, they both knew the end of the dream was in sight. For the first time in four hundred years, the vision of the future was clouded, almost as if someone had cloaked it. A cloud was gathering over Ireland and they knew it would bring hardship and death. William and Siobhan's dream had been sustained for four-hundred years. It was woven over and through every clan, family and Geraldine for hundreds of miles around but now something was causing it to fray.

London had long since grown impatient with the power of the Geraldines but now finally with the advent of Renaissance science they were able to do something about it.

Knowledge of ancient practices and formulas that had been outlawed by the church were revived and with the Reformation, gained the attention and empowerment under a Protestant English throne. Long suppressed for their knowledge and practice of the ancient teachings, the Knights of the Temple re-emerged in the guise of a Masonic secret society. Allied with the Faery Queen, Elizabeth Tudor and bent on revenge for the cruelty with which they were crushed by Rome, they vowed revenge and turned their attention on Catholic Ireland.

That century alone, the English had bloodied the Geraldines three times and now talk of genocide was in the air. Gerald's uncles had all been hanged for treason and Queen Elizabeth had captured and imprisoned him more than once. Now his wife Joan, the woman who kept the dream alive was dying and so was his ability to see the future.

Joan's son, Black Tom smirked as his hated adversary rode away with his mother in tow. He despised Gerald and his power, despised his Celtic ways. He despised his mother for marrying Gerald after his father's death and had personally betrayed him to the Elizabethans in an attempt to keep them apart. He vowed that one day he'd end the Geraldine dream forever, stamp it out and replace it with his own.

As he watched his mother slump in the saddle, drained from her efforts to keep the peace, he knew the end was coming fast and in a few short months his wish was made complete.

***

It rained that day the team of three black horses pulled Joan's funeral bier down the long winding road from Gerald's castle at Askeaton. It mixed with the tears as both knights and peasants mourned the procession, solemnly making its way toward the cemetery on the other side of the river. All seemed to know that something more than a person had died with Joan's passing. The Geraldines had lost control of their own dream.

Earl Gerald sensed it most of all and as he walked with Black Tom to the family vault where Joan's body was to rest, he knew that he, himself was the one to blame.

It was a sad ending to what had begun not far away at the sacred lake Gur, but there was little hope to recover the dream now. Joan was dead, laid to rest in her green dress as Black Tom plotted and Gerald stared into the dark.

Through the power of the Crusades and the return of the red stone, the Geraldines had exercised a nearly magical hold on the countryside for four-hundred years. But now, a new breed of men, of magicians with names like Dee, Sidney and Spencer had come to power in London and Gerald knew they would be coming for him.

These men had four hundred years to study the science of the stones and he knew they would be coming for the last remaining secrets of the Grail. So as the funeral ended and the darkness descended over the castle, he prepared for the long night, knowing that he would soon have to face his enemies, alone.

INTO THE NIGHT

"And how is Ireland the answer to creation through light?" I asked the strange young Simon as our train paused briefly at an English whistle-stop, to discharge passengers.

"Because Ireland is the origin of the Grail saga and the Grail saga is the clearest, living human metaphor of light's journey through dark matter as it finds its way back to its origin to complete the circuit." Simon Templar said, his eyes drawing to a squint.

"And how did you know to look there?" I asked, anxiously trying to find the nexus between my quest and Simon's quasi-scientific theories.

"I didn't." Simon said, as he shared a suspicious look with Jill. "I was helping a friend investigate some anomalies in the burials of Iron age Celts." He said quietly. "That's when my theory of light merged with an ontological reality and I realized I'd reached my depth."

The train picked up speed, rolling along through the English countryside, and as night descended Simon treated me and Jill to the discovery that had changed him from Christ's disciple to philosophical nomad.

"What was so unusual in the burials of Iron Age Celts?" I asked, as Jill turned an ear to the conversation.

"There weren't any." He said looking up at me with eyes that suddenly seemed lost beyond reason. "It's almost as if a space ship came down and picked up 300 years worth of men , women and children and just disappeared. So we came up with theories. A sudden fondness for cremation, a peculiar inclination to bury their dead in acidic soils which destroyed all trace. But none of the theories were consistent with their history or mythology."

"So where did they go?" I said, amazed that I'd never even heard the story before.

Simon paused as he looked nervously toward Jill. "Come outside," he said at last, as he motioned me toward the corridor.

I followed Simon for a full five minutes before we reached the nearly empty buffet car and claimed an end table.

"What's the big secret?" I asked.

"The guardians are always watching," Simon said glimpsing quickly over his shoulder. "They're everywhere. Look. This thing is science, mythology, UFOs, religion and national security all rolled into one and if you don't take it seriously fine. But the people responsible for keeping the secrets in this country and yours take it very seriously and those people are predominantly members of an ancient Babylonian secret society known as the Brotherhood. The Babylonian Brotherhood. But you probably know them as the Masons, the York Masons have a special role. Over a 300 year stretch of European history, beginning around one-fifty B.C., only Yorkshire shows evidence of traditional Celtic burials."

"Which means?" I asked, as Simon hesitated again, waiting to take the plunge.

"Which means, the Yorkshire Celts stayed behind to act as guardians."

"And Yorkshire Celts?" I asked, pursuing the string.

"Evolved into the Knights Templar and then into York Right Masons," he said, his voice showing the frustration. "And you can't be in British intelligence without being a York Right Mason! It's the great chain of command. Understand?"

I was beginning to. For years there was talk of a secret Masonic conspiracy intended to rule the world, but added to all the other alleged conspiracies of the century it seemed nothing more than talk. Then, with the sudden death of the new Pope John Paul and the election of the Polish Pope, John Paul II in 1978 something seemed to click. John Paul it seemed had been trying to get to the bottom of a seemingly incongruous scandal at the Vatican Bank, that involved an infiltration by a secret Masonic order known as the P2 lodge. It seemed that P2 had been more than active in counter-intelligence movements, drug smuggling and other illegal activities. A key figure, Italian banker Roberto Calvi had been found hanging from the Black friars Bridge in London, not a stone's throw from the old Templar church. But with the death of John Paul the scandal had seemed to disappear. Considering that membership in Masonry, a Medieval esoteric craft guild, was and still is forbidden by the church, the entire affair seemed to expose an incongruous riddle. As a freelance journalist I had made it my business to find out what that riddle was and it was one of the reasons I'd wound up in Afghanistan.

Afghanistan had been at the center of a plot to bring down the Soviet Union. Much of that plot required the surreptitious supply of weapons which were paid for by large quantities of illegal drugs, sold on the world market. But a more intriguing aspect to the plot relied on the mystical power of the Afghan freedom fighters to undo the mechanist Soviets. According to a Congressional report, it wasn't just Stinger missiles that had brought the Evil Empire down, it was something mystical and that something was shared by a secret—albeit—Masonic cabal within the intelligence community. Who these men were seemed to go back to the 1840's and Kipling's Masonic adventure story, the Man Who Would be King. But the roots of even that story had been much older and for the first time I was getting the connec tion to an ages-old plan.

"So where did they go? These Celts." I asked.

"They didn't go to France, I'll tell you that." Simon said, snorting out the answer. "My guess is they went to another dimension."

"C'mon my friend. I've seen and heard some wild things lately. But I think they'd lock you up for this," I said, unconvinced, but still fascinated by Simon's theory.

"The time period coincides to the Roman invasion exactly," Simon said, emphatically. "The Romans had been backing the Celts off the continent for over a hundred years. They'd finally reached Britain by fifty B.C., just about the end of the Iron age. News would have spread."

"But another dimension? Nobody just disappears." I said.

Simon shook his head in protest. "No, no. Celtic mythology is filled with talk of other worlds out of sync with our own. People would go there and come back not a day older, even though hundreds of years had passed."

"But that's pure mythology." I said in an attempt to dismiss the grandness of the scheme.

"Then why would the myths be taken so seriously by the Yorkshire men and why else would they be preparing the old sites like Stonehenge for their return?"

Simon's eyes took on a sudden glaze of hysteria and I had to admit, the idea knocked the wind out of me. "Their return?"

"Or our merger with them, whichever comes first. You heard the lady back there in the compartment. The walls between the dimensions are growing thin. One of these day, and I assume very soon, there won't be any walls at all." Simon said, squinting again as he wiped his glasses.

"And then what?" I asked.

"I don't know." He said. "But it frightens me."

Simon had woven a sort of scientific-mythological plot into one of the world's oldest intelligence services and done it very convincingly. There was no arguing that over the last four hundred years the British had become masters of the game of intelligence. It had all begun under the Elizabethans, when Sir Francis Walsingham employed writers like Christopher Marlowe and Edmund Spencer and courtiers like John Dee to weave the ancient knowledge in practical political policy and their descendants were still the masters of disguise.

There could be no telling over the centuries into whose life or business they had woven their intricate designs.

But there was at least one family that had proved to be the bane of their existence from the very beginning—one family whose knowledge of the secrets had clashed repeatedly with the interests of the Yorkshire men and their alliances. It was the Geraldines and now I was getting a clear idea exactly what that clash was about.

THE SCHOOL OF NIGHT

Even Rick seemed lost in time as Mary spun the background to the Geraldine Grail mysteries out before him. Like most, he'd had no idea of the esoteric jockeying and prolonged power struggle that had gone on long before the age of rationalism put blinkers on everyone's perception of what was real.

It was no wonder there had been such a need for secrecy. According to Mary, time was not endless, but finite. The entire millennium had been a race against time, and the key to time was the Grail. Whoever won the Grail got to claim nothing less than the door to eternity as their prize and in the twelfth century, the key to the Grail was Pembroke.

Pembroke, the Welsh city on the furthest, most westerly point of Britain had always maintained a strong mythic, almost magical connection to Ireland. Centuries before the coming of the Normans, the kingdom then known as Dyfed had been conquered by the Irish and it was from there the legends of Arthur and the Grail mysteries spread into Britain, France and Germany. Chretien de Troye had taken his Grail romances directly from the court bard, Bledri at Pembroke and Giraldus Cambrensis, the Geraldine author of Strongbow's conquest made Bledri a contemporary of Nest's.

Nest, mother of all Irish Geraldines had been a princess of this

Irish dynasty in Wales and the Norman Kings of England had been wise to keep an eye on this Celtic kingdom. According to legend, the Grail could never be restored without the cooperation of a royal line, which was what the sacred marriage, the Hieros Gamos had been intended to ensure. But after a thousand years as the end of time approached there was no telling what part of that line the Hieros Gamos would require.

It was no accident that upon the death of Strongbow in 1176, Henry II had passed the mystical Earldom on to his loyalist defender. William Marshal and his heirs had clamped the lid tightly on its Grail secrets for the next four hundred years. But with the final passing of the Marshal heirs, the Earldom again fell into friendlier hands and it is was then the lost secrets of the Grail and Strongbow's quest for it were rediscovered by occult philosophers.

The "School of Night" they called themselves. Edmund Spencer, author of the Fairy Queen; Walter Raleigh, conquistador, courtier and poet; John Dee, Elizabeth's astrologer and court magician; Mary Herbert, Countess of Pembroke and her brother Sir Philip Sidney, poet, occultist and holy warrior whose father Henry, was English governor of Ireland and whose father-in-law, Sir Francis Walsingham was Elizabeth's spymaster. The mystical past and the modern intel-ligence professional merged for the first time in the Elizabethan police state. It was the perfect marriage for seeking the Grail.

Using the secrets explained in Giordano Bruno's Christian Cabala these men and women would unravel the ancient texts and reassemble the puzzle according to their vision, then maintain it as a state secret. Here were the students whose understanding would secure the missing stones and birth an empire. With Elizabeth I as Monad, they would use their occult philosophy and the hidden powers of light to rule the world.

As they roamed through the ancient libraries and musty cellars of Pembroke, they uncovered what Strongbow had learned on his many adventures to Jerusalem; drawings of celestial hierarchies, access to the astral plane and all that lay beyond, hidden in the Sephiroth.

Throwing open the locked doors where the old texts were stored, they read of Alexander the Great and his possession of the lapis exilis, the small stone as large as an eyeball and of Strongbow's attempts to manufacture one by indulging in alchemy.

But even more importantly, they uncovered a lost book of Merlin prophecies interpreted by Giraldus Cambrensis, the Geraldine historian, and what they read made them bent on seizing the future.

"They know everything." Phillip Sydney said to the horror of his friends as they peered by candle light at the ancient scrolls, lying unread for centuries.

What Elizabeth's occultists found was what the Geraldines had known for four hundred years—the future. As a grandson of Nest, Cambrensis was intrigued with his Celtic heritage and as a priest, scholar and tutor to Henry's son, Prince John, he possessed the ability to travel and search out rare documents.

On an extensive trip through Wales he had persisted in finding an original copy of the prophecies of Merlin and eventually located one at the small village of Nefn on Caernarvon Bay.

Using his power as an officer of the King, he had taken the book and deciphered the language, intent on proving the prophecies applied to his sovereign Henry II, his Angevin sons and the great destiny they held for England.

But as Cambrensis decoded the text, that was by then nearly a thousand years old he came to see the Angevins in a different light and realized the prophecies were intended not for the king but for his own family of cousins and uncles now embroiled in a war for Ireland.

Frightened of the visions of the future the prophecies foretold, and fearful that the Cathar heretic Henry would bring them about if he understood their meaning, Cambrensis passed the prophecies along to his family. Then he stripped them from Strongbow's Conquest and withheld his promise of publication.

But what Cambrensis had successfully avoided with the Angevin kings Henry, Richard and John, the Elizabethan occultists now fulfilled.

On the face of the hard evidence the prophecies provided, it wasn't hard for Sidney to convince his father that the name Fitzgerald again meant "enemy" to everything they stood for and Lord Sidney's speech to the English Parliament was eloquent and to the point.

Over four hundred years, the Geraldines had fulfilled the Grail promise as the prophecies had predicted. Through clan connections and intermarriage, the Geraldine dream had grown to over a million of the most productive acres in Europe; farmland whose income alone exceeded the entire cost of England's administration of the island. It was a million acres that in Fitzgerald hands was untaxable and beyond the Pale.

The Geraldines were a constant reminder of the limits of English domain; rich, Catholic, independent and with the Counter Reformation threatening to overthrow Elizabeth, potential claimants to the throne of England. But more than that, if left unchecked, the Geraldine dream would eventually consume the millennium and this was something that would have to be stopped.

The only way out was all-out war, a war that would bring Ireland under the iron hand of English rule and save the stone kingdom from the Geraldines.

All the noble men as well as the nouveau mercantile class agreed. Ireland had no future in renegade Geraldine hands and only by waging God's holy war could that future be remade.

No mention was made, of course of the esoteric motives for Sidney's war or of the long, necromancing seances the Dee-Sidney-Pembroke circle conducted to revive the spirit of the dead Strongbow.

These "occult" practices for which Dee, Raleigh and the rest were eventually imprisoned were never discussed. But the war they conjured into existence with the help of Strongbow's ghost was a savage genocide.

Raleigh and Spencer were determined to wipe out the purpose from Gerald's race by cutting them off from their past and with the help of Gerald's enemies, a new dream was being made.

Black Tom Butler even led the assault on the vault where Joan, his mother lay. And as they dragged her body to the riverbank, hoisted it upon a cross and used it for target practice, he found himself totally without remorse.

But watching from the castle, high above the town, Gerald burned for revenge and as his heart broke, the ghosts of Siobhan and the Black Knight, like the spirits of life and death battled for his soul.

Tears flowed from Siobhan's ghostly eyes as the English musket balls pierced Joan's green dress, the one she and Gerald had been married in. But no amount of tears could hold back the message of the Black Knight as he whispered into Gerald's ear. "Follow me into the pool. Embrace the dark and be my tool."

Gerald heard the deep mournful cry of the Banshee, the death goddess of the Tuatha de Danaan as his mind snapped, his eyes riveted helplessly to the images of desecration before him. The countryside in ruins, much of his closest family dead or captured by the English, Gerald needed the Black Knight now, no matter what the wishes of his great ancestor had been.

Only the Black Knight, who had taken on the role of guardian of the stones by supplanting the dark monster of the pit, could muster the forces required to break the power now confronting him. Within the Black Knight was the simplicity of the war of light versus dark that would take the blood stone and protect it until it was safe to give forth it's magic of life again. Within the Black Knight's darkness was the power Gerald needed to fight, but he knew the price might mean his soul.

As night came to Askeaton, he snuck beneath the walls and rode to Lake Gur, near the castle of Crom Abu. It was a quiet, but beautiful place, a neolithic lake of sacrifice dedicated to the ancient gods, the Tuatha de Danaan. It was said that every seven years the lake went dry and revealed the Lady who lived beneath it. Anyone who was foolish enough to attempt to reach her was drowned by the onrushing waters and it was claimed one of Nest's own grandchildren had died there. The sacrifice of the young Gearoid Iarla to the ancient birth lake had wedded the Geraldines to the people of light, the Tuatha de Danaan—

and as Gerald dismounted and peered into its surface their spirits played out the past four hundred years before him.

There was the landing on the beach while Siobhan watched from the hill. There were the battles and the victories, the night William had struggled against the storm and his days with Siobhan in the sunshine. There was also the recent past; Gerald's imprisonment in London, the ghostly face of his wife Joan and the cloud of darkness that blacked out the future.

He touched the image to make it clear again, but instead the blackness took on form as if drawing power from the darkness of the lake. The valley seemed to echo with the sound of voices and as Gerald turned he found himself face to face with the Black Knight, the red bloodstone gripped firmly in his hand.

After all these years it still pulsed with a brilliance that seemed to animate and give life to this ancestor of the Geraldines. For the first time in four-hundred years a child of Nest was confronting the darkness from where he'd come—in the birth lake of his family's dreams, and in his need was about to be reborn from it.

"Don't you love me the best?" The Black Knight asked in a voice that sounded of broken glass.

"Who are you?" Earl Gerald asked as he stared into his eyes.

"I am what you've been and what you are about to become," he said reaching out toward Gerald.

***

I awoke in the cramped compartment of the train, my companion Jill, staring at me with her violet eyes. Whatever Simon's paranoia about spies or theories of "beings of light," it was reassuring to know we could take on such pleasant forms.

Whoever it was we were, my dream of the Black Knight was drawing closer to me now, his shadow hovering nearby and as the train whistle screamed out the approach of the last station, I shook myself awake.

"Where are we?"

"On our way to Ireland," Jill said, smiling as she lifted a long delicate arm to retrieve her bag from overhead.

"You're going there too?" I stammered, still groggy from the dream.

"To places no one else can go. Want to come?" She said seductively, intentionally pressing her long body closer to mine as she lowered her bag.

Staring at a doleful Simon for a moment, I wondered if Jill wasn't some wonderful spy, somehow sent to dream her way into my dreams and report back to the Temple in London on how my progress was coming.

But as I lost myself in the smell of her perfume, her breasts gently rocking to the motion of the train, my paranoia faded. And as she bent low to whisper in my ear, "I know it's what you want." Simon's warnings disappeared.

ILLUSION

Rick stared at the crystal on Mary's table and touched it cautiously, almost as if to make sure it was real. The December darkness outside threw long shadows over her pictures of the royals and artifacts from the past and for the first time he felt somehow as if the woman did possess a power to make them come alive.

He shivered. "So if this whole business goes back to the First Crusade and this young knight taking on the role of a Grail guardian, why has Paul been drawn into it?"

"Because Paul is completing the last and final phase of the understanding before the cycle ends. He is passing it from dream to reality, picking up all the lost pieces and making sense of them, no matter how scattered. You see, when time ends, the light must have penetrated the darkness completely which is why the Black Knight has been seeking Paul out. They must forge an understanding."

Alissa looked to Rick, holding back the feeling of growing terror.

"A lot of very religious people know about the war of the Light against the Dark, but very few of them are the descendants of a real Black Knight. In truth, of all the knighthoods the Geraldines have possessed, only the Black knighthood remains and only if Paul completes his journey, can he be released from the darkness," Mary said in a quiet voice.

"If he completes it?" Alissa asked, her voice trembling.

"The progress of the Black Knight was stopped by the Elizabethans when they killed the fourteenth and last Earl of the Desmond. They captured him. If your father can reach back and remember his purpose—live it with him and process his feelings, the darkness of our present world can be undone. If he cannot, the war of the Light against the Dark will continue. I needn't tell you Mr. Kendall with all your moment-to-moment news analysis where all that is leading."

Alissa agreed. "It was in my father's book the Apostle's Diary." She explained to Rick. "The fourteenth Earl invoked the power of the Black Knight. Rome gave him a document known as the Just War Doctrine to conduct a holy war against the Elizabethans. Ronald Reagan used it to justify the use of nuclear weapons for fighting wars and if Ronald Reagan can use it . . . . "

Rick shook his head in disbelief. "How do we resolve this?"

"We'll have to wait and see. I'm sure Paul must be trying very hard," Mary said wryly as Alissa's face turned grim. "Don't worry my dear. If he does it, you'll be the first to know."

***

Outside, Rick found himself more confused than ever.

"So where do we go from here?" He asked as he escorted Alissa down the busy Soho street.

"Are you really interested now? Or is this still just part of the deal?"

"I guess I'm finally catching up," he said. "I just never appreciated what happened before—the way I do now, the mythology, the play of forces . . . . "

"It's all a dream Rick," Alissa said, stopping to stare into Rick's eyes. "The only question is whose dream is it?"

The two stared for a long moment, nervously glancing as each waited for the other to make the next move. To Alissa, Rick actually seemed humbled for the first time and as they walked, she began to feel the first creeping feelings of trust.

"Look. Come back to my office and I'll show you what we do there," Rick said, bundling himself up against the winter chill.

Alissa pulled back. "I don't think so."

"Oh C'mon. You've dragged me to museums and mediums, you've shown me the past, the least you can do is let me show you the future."

"My father would love to hear you say that!" Alissa said sarcastically.

"O.K. then. One possible future," Rick said, as he threw his hands up in exasperation. "Please? You'd be amazed at what our hardware geeks can do."

***

Alissa was generally unimpressed with the huge chrome and glass facade of the Transitron building. In many ways, it didn't even seem like a building as much as a giant antenna, stretching up into the heavens to catch whatever signals might stray into its path. Even the long corrugated steel corridors that led to the basement seemed like conductors, laid out like huge circuits ferrying human ideas along the miles of cable, back and forth from the surface to the depths below.

"What do they do down here?" Alissa asked as they passed a series of glassed-in rooms on either side of the corridor.

"These are environment rooms where we experiment with new ideas. I showed your father the technology the day he was in to see me."

"But there's nothing here," Alissa said.

Rick entered one of the viewing rooms and walked to a control panel buried in the wall. Fiddling with the panel, the room suddenly became a three dimensional hologram of a 1930's Hollywood musical, filled with a buzz of people.

"Wow," Alissa said. "How do you do that?"

"The computers you saw upstairs record the images, which are essentially two dimensional and assign three dimensional values to each character. "It looks great, but it's just a three dimensional picture really," he said, waving his hand through a dancing chorus girl with bobbed blond hair.

"Virtual reality doesn't get much better than this, but the goal is total immersion. Up until recently, the computing speed hasn't been available to do that but, as I ex plained to your father we had a kind of breakthrough with the latest version."

"Where the body actually makes up for what the computer can't do?" Alissa said, moving to the console and examining the case of eyeball size crystals stacked neatly on top of one another.

"Exactly. There's only a subtle difference in the electronics but it makes for a qualitative change. It appears reality is maintained by the subject. Everything you see, hear and feel relies on this," Rick said, pointing to his head. "If you alter the perception of reality, you can alter the reality."

"That's a little frightening," Alissa said, removing one of the crystals from the box and removing a Dream Catcher from the shelf. "What'll this do?"

"Oh. That's a reality module for the Dream Catcher. You need the chips to get the whole effect, but your father would kill me if I let you . . ."

Without asking, Alissa dropped the crystal into the little black machine and in an instant the happy-go-lucky Hollywood movie was gone—replaced by a darkened Cathedral.

Like a huge black drape had suddenly been drawn over the room, Alissa shuddered and as the room filled with the sound of marching feet and the sight of black armor clad soldiers, she panicked.

"Rick. What is this?" She screamed from the other side of what was now a Cathedral. "I can't see you."

"I'm over here." Rick shouted as he made his way across a room now populated by the same frightening holographic beings Paul had witnessed in the Templar church.

"What is this program?" Alissa asked, cowering into the recesses of the Cathedral.

"We hired a bunch of Hollywood types to create realistic environments for us to plug into. But I don't remember this one," Rick said peering into the scene as Paul suddenly materialized from out of nowhere.

"What in blazes?" Rick said, as a voice called out from behind.

"It's dangerous coming down here unscheduled," a young tech, in lab coat and glasses said as he walked through the maze of holograms and switched off the power causing the images to fold up and disappear.

"What was that?" Rick asked, as his eyes adjusted to the sudden shift of images.

"Something Lord Gilbert cooked up for fun. He's goofy for all that Medieval stuff. Who's this?" The man asked, again standing in an empty room.

Rick was guarded. "A friend. Alissa, this is our resident technical genius Malcolm."

Malcolm paused as he surveyed Alissa through his thick glasses, then motioned them outside.

"How did that guy get into the hologram?" Rick asked, as they followed Malcolm to his work room.

"The guy standing in the middle, just then? I assume Lord Gilbert put him there."

Alissa reacted, angrily. "But he's not an actor."

"Yea, well." Malcolm said, shuffling his feet guiltily. "Lord Gilbert's a pretty clever guy. Maybe he beamed him in from outer space."

Alissa eyed Rick. "Need I say more?"

"Not right now!" Rick answered coldly as he turned his attention to the technician. "What did you find out about the whiteouts?"

"The contact is being directed from inside the building all right. But it's not electronic. I mean it's electronic in that the signal is a wave, but it's lacking any known man made signature, like a circuit."

Rick's mouth dropped. "How is that possible?"

The tech scanned the room. "In this realm anything is possible. Reality here is all just a matter of frequencies and what you do with them. Look at this."

Malcolm flipped a switch on an oscilloscope and in an instant the screen filled with wavy white lines. "I grabbed the last bunch of whiteouts and ran them through the processor."

"So what is it?" Rick asked.

"A very long wave that seems to be moving into our spectrum."

"Say again?"

"Everything we do, TV, radio, microwave ovens, computers modulates within a given set of frequencies. Each one of them has a duration, short to long. This wave is so long, from our perspective it doesn't even look like a wave, it just looks like this huge band of white noise."

"Like a tidal wave?" Alissa asked, peering into the growing mass of white lines on the occiliscope.

"Like a tsunami!" Malcolm said, his eyes widening for emphasis. "I don't know where this thing is coming from or what it is. But its like, if we're at sea level, this wave is three hundred feet deep and climbing."

"So where's the interference?

"Right here along this line," he said pointing to the curve of the graph. Something coming out of this building has been intersecting it through our net. Every time it rubs up against it, the energy flowback is so huge it overloads us and shuts us down. The rest of the net hasn't even touched it yet. But if it actually comes in any closer I don't know what's going to happen."

"Maybe then we'll all wake up," Alissa said, as she peered down into the screen then turned toward Rick. "Into the new dream."

LORD GILBERT

"You told us we could ride the wave. Ride it, you said. If we just gave you enough time and money. Well, we're running out of both." Lord Sidney complained from one end of the board room as he pounded his fist on the round table. "Were we fools to have followed you for so long? You said we could preserve things just the way we are and get the Grail of knowledge at the same time. But this dimension is breaking down around us as we speak."

"My promise and the promise of my father was to build an electronic cocoon that would allow us to continue on in our present form seamlessly past the end of time. Gentlemen we have succeeded in doing that."

"Lord Gilbert. I am aware of your promises and your immense abilities in this matter, but only this morning I was greeted on my way to work by a band of dwarves ... "

"Piskies, I believe is the proper term, Sir Sydney," another board member chimed in.

"Piskies then," Sir Sydney continued, growing exasperated. "Whatever you call them, I'm expecting a flying saucer to greet me on the way home. We have to stop this."

Lord Gilbert remained calm. "In just a matter of hours, our final engineering sta tions will go on-line, turning all communication on the planet from analog to digital. In that form, no matter what the strength of the signal or the duration of the wave that is about to wash over us we can shield our dimension from absorption. We can pick and choose from the new paradigm, but through the digital electronics we'll still remain in control," Lord Gilbert answered confidently.

"But are you sure it will work?" Lord DeBurgo replied. "The geometry of Solomon's Temple didn't work very well for the Jews two-thousand years ago. What makes you think its magic will work now?"

"The priests of Solomon's Temple were caretakers. If Solomon had our electronics, the Romans wouldn't have had a chance. Solomon's Temple was lacking in technology. My machines can duplicate the spectrum, maintain a world in fullest bloom and deepest color and maintain that dream forever, our dream."

Gilbert bragged, jamming his finger into the table as an assistant crept to his side and whispered in his ear.

"But what about the Geraldine dream? I know we've taken care of the important ones. But there are still plenty of them out there. And you know we never did find their pieces of the puzzle," DeBurgo continued.

"Rest assured gentlemen. The Geraldine dream is mine and mine alone. There is nothing they know that I soon won't and nothing they can do that I can't override. By the time the wave is here I'll have whatever pieces of the puzzle I need and the rest I can make up from here."

"But what if there are others who share a different dream?" Lord Sidney asked. "Are you absolutely sure you can contain them and prevent them from interfering?"

"We have always contained the enemy, Sir Sidney and we have more resources than ever at out disposal. It's that simple."

Lord Gilbert dismissed Sidney with a wave of his hand then smiled. "Gentlemen, we have a visitor."

Instantly the thick double doors opened revealing Rick and Alissa, surprised to see such a late night meeting underway.

"My dear Richard, I had no idea you were romantically involved," Gilbert said, jokingly.

Embarrassed before the board, Rick scrambled to try and explain.

"Lord Gilbert this is Paul's daughter, Alissa Fitzgerald. I was just giving her a tour when I heard the voices coming from the room."

Gilbert stood quickly, framed by the lighted Millennium Wheel outside the window.

"Alissa. It is a pleasure," he said, grabbing her hand. "I so look forward to working with your father in the future."

Alissa smiled grimly but said nothing as Lord Gilbert draped a long, ape-like arm possessively around her shoulder.

"In fact I think it was wonderful of Mr. Kendall bringing you here for the rest of us to meet. I had no idea he was so resourceful."

"I really have to go," Alissa said as she slowly peeled Lord Gilbert's arm away from her shoulder.

"Then let my driver take you home while I meet with Mr. Kendall. Now that you've brought him here I've remembered there are a thousand things I need to speak to him about."

Gilbert's smile turned to anger as Alissa was ushered from the room, leaving Rick alone standing by his desk.

"What in the name of St. Blaize did you bring her here for?" Gilbert ranted, suddenly turning from the genteel diplomat to a raging gorilla.

"Someone broke into her apartment. She thought it might be us searching for her father's book," Rick said, holding his ground. "I thought it might be a good idea to show her around, convince her that a man like you would never condone such actions."

Gilbert's rage cooled.

"You did the right thing, Rick. I'm sorry I grew angry. Have you had any luck?"

"I haven't been able to locate him," Rick said, staring blankly at Lord Gilbert.

Lord Gilbert turned and walked back to his seat at the table. "I know where he is. I meant with the book."

"You know where he is?" Rick responded, now truly surprised. How?"

"If you don't know the truth, then you don't have to lie." Gilbert said, a look beyond cynicism creeping over his face. "Have you forgotten the first maxim of the news business?"

Glaring at the board, Rick showed his anger at being used and walked to the opposite side of the round table to face Lord Gilbert directly. "You mean, you don't trust me to lie for you?"

"Of course I trust you to lie, Richard." Gilbert said to assorted chuckles from his peers. "I'm simply concerned that a man in your position needs to lie believably. Appearances are everything my boy. It's the frontage, the image that people respond to, not the idea. And as long as you control it. You can get away with absolutely anything."

"Even the Grail?" Rick said, looking around at the odd lot of men huddled around the table.

Gilbert smiled in real surprise, almost as if he'd underestimated Rick.

"The Grail, is it? Why, I'm happy to see you're finally connecting with our purpose," he said admiringly. "Of course the Grail. What did you think all this was for? You think I actually like reruns of I Love Lucy or transferring people's telephone calls? Did you think we developed all this so some sun-tanned cow, half-way 'round the world could sit by her pool and order up a frozen pizza?"

"I don't think I ever really thought about it until today. So it's all just a means to an end. The asinine programming, the satellite service, the unrelenting drive for technology, the escalating fees all paid for this moment."

The other board members eyed Lord Gilbert with varying degrees of curiosity as his face suddenly turned sad. By the look in his eyes he had waited a long time for this and as he turned away from Rick, he seemed to sigh. "Yes!"

THE TRAVIS INN

The crossing from Bristol had brought us to Hotel near Dublin with little time left to sleep. Simon was getting to me now and I wanted to know more.

"So, you deduced a connection between these missing Celts and some dimensional crossover. But you never told me how that lead you to Ireland." I said, as we camped out by the fire in the hotel's small pub.

Simon nervously adjusted his glasses, then reached into his pocket and pulled out a handful of glass balls of various sizes and colors. "We started finding these where the Celts should have been. Vast piles of them. At first we thought they were just uncut beads. Then I heard about the mansion of Angus at New Grange, a place called Bru Oengusa by the Irish."

Simon withdrew a piece of paper from his pocket with a chalk rubbing of signs and swirls. "This design" he said, pointing to the paper, . . . "the triple swirl and consecutive interlocking triangles? It's not art. It's a working diagram."

"Of what?" I asked.

"Accessing the frequencies of the cosmos in order to control time—or as some of us believe—accessing the Grail. We've cross-referenced the mythologies to all the scientific data. This stuff comes out of the dark past, long before the pyramids. But we're just realizing how advanced it is. Ever hear of Chaco Canyon in New Mexico? 12th century, 1100's—the Chaco had these all over the place. You could basically guide a star ship through the galaxy they measured time so accurately and their descendants claim they could control nature with their secret technology. New Grange, the mansion of Angus is 5,000 years older and that makes it the Grail Castle. There's no doubting it."

I examined the glass beads, if that was what they were. It was uncanny how they resembled the Dream Catcher. "Over 6000 years old, you say? How do I find this place?"

Simon smiled nervously and checked his watch. "I'm leaving in about 20 minutes. Tag along if you like."

***

Most of the road North to Drogheda was highway now, the narrow cow path that William of Orange had used to bring in his Protestant holy warriors in 1688, long since widened and paved over. But even four hundred years later, the wreckage of the invasion could still be seen.

The original army of Anglo-Norman invaders that had come with the Geraldines in 1170; the de Lacys, de Courcis, de Ridenfords and de Prendergasts, Montmaurices, FitzStephens and FitzHenrys had formed a layer of feudal aristocracy that had remained much intact long after feudalism had passed its prime on the Continent.

That layer had wedded itself to Irish ways and Irish life and as the armies of Orange moved in, it had become the object of wrath and destruction.

You could still view the broken castles and burned manor houses sitting in the fields, their once proud owners as vanished as the Celtic way of life they sought to protect.

"Do you ever get the feeling you've passed this way before?" I asked as I stared out at the ruins.

"All the time." Simon replied, as if expecting the question. "But it was a long time ago."

"Then what are we doing here again?" I asked.

"Finishing the loose ends. Putting the last pieces into the puzzle."

"But what is the puzzle?"

For the first time since we met, Simon smiled. "The Sufis spend a lot of time on that question. Alam almithal, that's what their name for the big "what" is. Some say it's a dream, some say it's thought, others call it the country of the hidden Imam. It's what all life is, one big dream."

"Then who's the dreamer, you or me?"

Simon stared at the road ahead. "The plane of existence was created by the dreams of many people, not just one."

"But what if it was just one?" I said.

Simon was quiet, content to focus his gaze onto the dark road beyond.

It reminded me of Afghanistan, driving through the mountains at night. The mountains of Afghanistan were the home of Sufi mysticism, what the twelfth-century Persian Sohrawardi called Na-Koja-Abad or the land of nonwhere. Out of that land where the spirits dwelled came our reality and for some reason Afghanistan had remained opened like a door to it through its long history.

Alexander the Great had walked through that door looking for the lapis exilis, the stone that would show him the future. By cutting the Gordian knot he'd created the West, but severed the West from the source of its dream and so it was left to Charlemagne's Frankish Knights to find it again and so they did, hidden in a basement tomb in Jerusalem.

I found it strange how without even knowing the mythology of the Grail quest, its symbols had shown up in my dreams. The Black Knights were the guardians of time, one hundred and fifty two knights empowered to ensure the dream's survival from millennium to millennium. But at the end of time, a one hundred and fifty-third knight was to come along. When that time came, his one dream would lead everyone to the Grail of existence and the end of everything we knew to be real. 153, the sum of the integers between 1 and 17. 117, 1170. Added together they all made 9, no matter how you tried and 9 was the number of the great goddess, the female matrix, the mother of creation Isis, Semiramis, Mary.

"My friends and I have been getting together here every year since the millennium." Simon said, as the sky began to brighten.

"On the winter solstice?"

"On the three darkest mornings. It's a sight to see when the light first hits the quartz crystals. Like some huge clock, the sun throws a 17 centimeter shaft of light for exactly 17 minutes."

"17 minutes. As you said, that fits the mythologies."

Simon was almost giddy. "It's consistent with the geometry of the pyramids. The Great flood began on the 17th day of the 7th month. The name of God has 17 letters and at the end of time 17 prophets will be born, each bearing one letter of his name. That's 1 and 17."

"And that adds up to 153." I said.

Simon looked over at me. "So you know what I'm talking about."

"I know what the numbers do. I know what some people believe they mean. I'm not sure I want to believe it."

"You have to believe it. It's a technology we're talking about—synchronizing the power of the universe to matter here on earth. Call it Geomancy, call it the divine providence, call it anything you want. Something brought us here to this reality and I believe this is how we get out." Simon said.

"But where do we go from here?"

Simon pointed to a glowing egg shaped mound rising in the distance. "I have no idea, but there's the Grail Castle. Maybe today's the day we finally find out."

It wasn't until we rounded the bend and I saw the Bru from the front that I understood what Simon meant. New Grange, Bru Oengusa, Bru na Boinn was a neo lithic "passage grave" built onto the top of the highest hill in the area. At least six thousand years old, the Bru was the home of the Dagda, the father god of the Tuatha de Danaan. According to the famous mythologist Joseph Campbell, that fact made the Bru the very home of the Dagda's bowl, a mythological concept now accepted by scholars as the origin of British and European Grail legends.

For centuries, the Grail castle had stood as an enigma in Western mythology and the construction of the Bru was nothing less than enigmatic. Seventy-eight and a half meters long by eighty-three and a third meters wide, the huge egg-shaped dome's surface was lined with quartz crystal and glowed like some huge solar-powered time machine.

The Bru had been left standing in the middle of the richest of rich farmland in Ireland, unopened and unappreciated for millennia. While the ghosts of the Tuatha de Danaan slept unmolested inside, cows grazed casually without.

But following England's final conquest of Ireland at the nearby "Battle of the Boyne," the tomb was broken open and for over two hundred years, viewed with a mixture of confusion and suspicion by noted British antiquarians. Displaying an unusual hatred for the local population, they mostly rejected the very idea that the structure could even be Irish, attributing the design to no less than wandering Egyptians, East Indians, Ethiopians, or Phoenicians. But as we entered the twenty-first century, the age of cyberspace and fiber optics, the Bru took on a uniquely Irish, "Otherworldly" identity.

People were already gathering as Simon pulled the car into the parking lot. Together we filed up the long, torch lit hill, one by one, steam billowing from our breaths into the frosty air.

At the top the crowd swelled to a hundred or more devotees and as Simon turned toward me holding one of the glass beads in his hand, my head began to spin again. "This area is filled with passage graves" he said. "But everyone is drawn to this one. I've managed to be inside when the sun hits tomorrow. But Bru Oengusa is so amazing I had to see it on the very first day."

A cheer went up as the first rays of light broke over the horizon and within seconds lit up the dimly glowing egg like a bright white quartz mother ship from outer space.

"And even as he spoke, the light began to glow and pervade the cave and to melt the earthen floor into itself like a fiery sun. And there was everywhere a wandering ecstasy in the sound ... Do you get the picture?" Simon said as the crowd began to chant and sway to the rhythm of Gaelic song.

"I do," I whispered as I tried to balance myself. But the spinning was as bad as the day at the Templar Church and the more I struggled, the more I seemed drawn into the chanting swirl. Something primal was happening to me, the smoke and sweat making me at one with the knowledge of the cosmos, winding me in and out like a strand of DNA—the quartz light piercing my mind. It was easy now to understand the intent of the Dagda. How the mythologies of his Grail mansion were a primal source for the mysticism of Buddhism, Islam, and medieval Christian heresies.

Pilgrims had come here from as far away as ancient Rome to commune with the spirits of the Dagda, to dance along side his family of gods and goddesses at the winter solstice and watch the ground melt away before them. How could they have known how to use the power inherent in the place—in their minds? How could we have so forgotten. I struggled toward the elaborate curb stones with their triple spiral swirls and felt them with my fingers. There were pockets there, indentations just large enough for a marble, or maybe a glass aggie.

Simon had been right about one thing. The symbols did mean something. But attached as they were to such an elaborate quartz instrument as the Bru, I considered the symbols might be more than just an instruction manual.

I reached for the small glass Dream Catcher aggie and fitted it into one of the many junctions that joined in an X. Like a key in an old lock, it seemed a perfect fit, almost too perfect and in an instant, the world dropped away.

As if standing in the center of a huge vortex I viewed the world as it revolved around me—all time and place as one inside the giant hologram. Here was the young Irish farm girl Siobhan and her Black Knight lover, William. There was the battle of Ossary and the mad king Dermot. Over there was Strongbow making love to his fiery Brigit.

I watched their faces. And as Siobhan placed the clear red stone into the pocket of the complex geometric swirls I found myself beyond time.

Like so much of what had been happening to me since Afghanistan, there was no explaining this in rational terms. For some reason, due to my ancestry I was being hunted down, pursued and watched from morning until night and even in my dreams I had gone on-line. The optics contained in the Transitron crystal had opened my mind to a world of multi-dimensional thought and as time neared its end, I could feel immersed in that world. It was exactly as Jill had said. The fabric was breaking down. Thought and desire were merging into one. But as the images closed in around me, I could feel a terror approaching and as the red stone danced before my eyes, I knew the confrontation I feared most had finally arrived.

FIRES WHICH BURNT BRIGHTLY

"Where am I?" I asked the image that suddenly transformed into a set of ruby red lips.

"Safe with me, back at the Inn." Jill replied, as she pressed a cold towel to my head. "You passed out. That strange young man in black, the minister returned you here. He said he hoped you'd feel better soon."

"I don't remember anything. I just remember following a red stone."

"Why that sounds like my experience. Come to think of it, there was a red stone in my crossover dream too."

My head hurt. "Crossover? Is that what I've done? Have I crossed over?"

"The first one is the most difficult. It gets much easier. The vertigo goes away. You begin to enjoy it." Jill said, soothingly.

"Is this what they call the mysteries?"

Jill's face glowed with a mellow excitement.

"Ever since you went to Afghanistan you have approached Aryana. As you have learned there are many obstacles to overcome."

"Like the Black Knight," I asked.

"The Black Knight is the first and last male guardian of the tree of life. The progress of his soul is to experience all life, fight all battles and suffer all indignities in order that he may equal the female as a partner, not a keeper." Jill ran her fingers gently across my forehead. "You shouldn't be surprised that he would lead you to me."

"I could use an explanation." I said, trying to lift myself from the bed.

"As we grow closer to the destination point in time, the dimension we live in is absorbed into other dimensions. When that happens, our sense of time and space, everything will change. But the transition won't be all at once. In fact, the transfer has been happening gradually for years but in ways people wouldn't notice. Then, one day soon, when the winter Solstice shines its first rays of light over the horizon, a catabolic reaction will occur. It's coming soon." Jill sat quietly for a moment, here eyes gazing lazily.

"Does it have a name?"

"It has many names. There are many worlds; worlds beyond your imagination. Some are near, surrounding us on the astral plane, whispering in our dreams. Others are far off in distant galaxies, waiting, hoping for us to visit them so they can teach us their wisdom," she said calmly, unbuttoning the top buttons of her knit dress. "But up until now all have remained unknown, except to the initiate."

"How did you learn about this?" I asked, watching the glow from the fireplace dance in Jill's eyes.

Jill smiled seductively then placed her hands over her belly, the slight curve off which could be seen through her knit dress. "Agape. The Indian women of South America taught me to use my womb."

"I don't understand."

"Not surprising," Jill added, hungrily sliding her outstretched fingers down her belly, until they reached the crest of her groin. "Can't have people knowing creation machines that incarnate spirit into this world can disincarnate them as well. Can we?"

Jill leaned over the table, the scent of her perfume causing my head to spin again. "Imagine a world where sex and religion were the same. A whole system of worship where women initiated men into the secrets of the many worlds and kept them connected."

I took a deep breath. "I'm trying," I said, now drawn in, body and soul as Jill's powerful spell washed over me.

"Then close your eyes and remember the first time you felt desire for a woman."

My head spun as Jill reached across the table and placed her hands on my face, filling me with her scent.

"You wanted to hold her, feel her, smell her hair. Do you remember that feeling, that sensual excitement that you felt? That is the energy that guides you. That's the power."

The color rose in Jill's cheeks as I took her hands.

"Feel it," she said, pulling my hands to her and holding them against her soft belly. "Find it within me."

I said nothing as the long and beautiful woman suddenly rose, then walked toward the dresser where she slowly slipped out of her dress and let it fall to the floor. I was filled with her now. But something was wrong as I found myself fighting a growing sense of anger.

"Something's not right," I said as Jill stood half naked before me, arms crossed against her breasts, a sheer slip hanging from her hips.

"You're not afraid?" She asked, tauntingly.

"Not for me," I whispered, the words whistling through my clenched teeth. "I'm afraid for you."

Outside, the storm finally burst and as I watched the rain and lightning reflect through the window, I struggled to come to grips with the anger.

"Don't be afraid for me." Jill said, in a voice that was nearly mocking. "I can take care of myself. Just as long as you believe in the dream. Believe in the power of creation."

Jill dropped her arms to her side and walked to the bed, gently moving her long frame to my side. "Come to me Paul. Come and I will teach you the mysteries of death and resurrection."

I was tormented by the feelings, but the sight of Jill was too much to resist. And as I reached out, her breasts gently swaying in the firelight, she smiled.

***

Lord Gilbert stared out at the Millennium Wheel from his office window as he cradled the antique box in his hands. It had been a present from his father, the box, passed down generation after generation and venerated almost as a holy relic. It was a holy relic, carrying within it a raw mystical power of the seer, long since suppressed for public consumption but held in secret by a brotherhood of Crusaders.

Now as he opened the box, light again emanated from the inside and as he reached down to withdraw the contents it seemed to fill the room with a powerful glow.

"Oh Semiramis, Queen of the Night. Hear my plea. Let me worship as your humble servant. I grovel at your feet and have longed for you to join with me. Be mine oh Queen. Give me the power of your mighty throne and I shall restore to you the power you once knew."

Lord Gilbert's face was illuminated as he drifted into a trance, the room growing brighter by the second. The monitor wall blinked on and off furiously as the energy surged through him.

***

I was dreaming with her now, tossing and turning on the bed as Jill lay beside me, arms crossed regally over her breasts like an Egyptian queen. Again, I beheld the face of Siobhan, her silky voice beckoning me from beyond as we raced through golden fields under an azure sky of deepest summer. "Come to me Paul. Come to me now" she said, her voice like music.

But as I struggled to catch her and pull her to my side, I saw the loving smile go blank. And as the image faded, Siobhan became the face of Jill and Jill became the viper.

"Come to me!" She seemed to belch in a voice that resonated like the bubbling of a tar pit. "Come to me now" she said, as her lips became a hungry gorge and her smile a Cobra's smile.

THE HORROR

The last thing I remembered was the tortured face of Jill, spent and burned as she lay atop a blazing fire, her mission, along with her lithe body, curling into the sky in wisps of smoke. I could barely move as I dragged myself off the bed and staggered to the dresser, now lit by bolts of lightning from the raging storm outside.

I stared into the mirror and tried to concentrate of where I was—Ireland, the night before the Solstice. Then I saw the glass balls that Simon had brought with him to Bru Oengusa, the Mansion of Angus lying on the dresser. They were different now, slightly changed in color, glowing with a flickering light. And as I glared at them closely I heard a faint scream. Inside the glass, peering out from within was the image of Jill, trapped inside the dream forever.

My mind froze, but as I dropped them to the floor I realized my nightmare was just beginning. "Don't you love me the best?" The Black Knight said as he stepped in from the storm.

"What did you do with that woman?" I snapped as he stood blocking the doorway, his armor hissing from the rain.

"If that's what she was," he answered in that crushed glass voice.

"What do you mean?" I asked. "I needed her to finish what I started."

"You don't need the enemy. The enemy needs you."

"Then what am I supposed to do?"

"Follow me," the Black Knight answered, turning toward the courtyard. "Into the West. Into the past."

Two horses, one white, one black stood in the courtyard waiting as we mounted up and rode off into the stormy night.

The air was cold and as we broke from the roadway and into the countryside, my head cleared.

"Where is this place?" I asked, stopping by a beautiful valley as the sun rose over the ruins of a castle.

"Castle Crom," The Black Knight replied as voices echoed up from the valley floor, faintly at first then growing into a chant. "A long time ago."

"Aboo, Aboo, Aboo," the voices called as the morning mists cleared, revealing thousands of Irish peasants swarming through the valley toward an oncoming army of Elizabethan soldiers.

"It's the dream of Gerald, the last Earl," I said as I watched the battle unfold.

"It's the dream as Gerald," the Black Knight answered as we watched Sir Walter Raleigh's army of musketeers form up lines on the other side of the valley. Raleigh and Edmund Spencer smiled knowingly as their battalions of Protestant mercenaries armed their muskets and cannons and prepared for battle.

"Haboo? What is this Haboo?" An addled old senior officer asked of the two young dandies as they sat astride their horses waiting for the slaughter.

"Hubbub, my Lord. Hubbub. These Irish use it when they go to war," Spencer replied sharing the joke with the young Raleigh.

I stared grimly as the scene unfolded, knowing what was to come. "I know how the battle turns out. I know we lose this war. Why are you showing me this?" I asked of the Black Knight.

"Because you need to remember," he said as he suddenly brought his mailed fist down hard on the rump of my horse.

The blow sent me galloping into the middle of the developing battle just the way my dreams back in London had sent me to Ireland and then the Crusades. So immersed, for a moment I even thought I could make a difference as the forces rallied behind me, armed with pitchforks and rusty swords. But nothing was going to change history as row upon row of Elizabethan muskets rained down, leaving me alone in a smoking mass of death with no option but to run.

I raced to the spot where the Black Knight sat perched atop a hill. "How could you let them die?" I asked, as he calmly watched the English soldiers finish off the wounded with their swords and knives. "I embraced you. And this is what you delivered?"

"All must be tested before the judgement day" he said.

"That's not an answer!" I demanded.

"All must be known and understood," he continued, coldly. "You came to me for the truth. I am here to ensure you receive it."

"Don't you think I know?" I yelled, my mind racing back and forth over the centuries. "Don't you think I've felt their anguish, all of their anguish all my life? That's my family being slaughtered down there, in their own valley. Your family. Don't you think I know the truth?"

The Black Knight stared without emotion. "Not yet, but soon."

My heart sank as I stared at this pitiless black thing, but I did understand his job. The Black Knight was the ultimate defender whose judgements were a simple black or white. He knew nothing of subtleties, only the truth and the lie and only when his truth was known, could the power of the lie be banished and the Grail achieved.

"Then let's get on with it." I said as that truth sank in.

I followed the Black Knight through the countryside of Desmond, now ravaged and deserted from almost twenty-five years of war. I watched as starving peasants bolted in fear as we approached. "Why do they run?" I asked.

"Because you are a ghost," the Black Knight replied coldly as he spurred his horse along. "You are their terror."

Weathered bones still clung to rusted swords as we passed along mile after mile, from battlefield to battlefield where the skeletons of entire armies still lay where they had fallen. Nearly half the population of Ireland had disappeared during the Desmond war in a genocide which by its end, had the fourteenth Earl, Gerald fighting on singlehandedly. Even Raleigh and Spencer's own accounts of the atrocities went long unpublished, suppressed for generations by a government in London afraid that its barbarism in seizing Ireland would undermine the appearance of its moral authority.

But none of it mattered to the Black Knight. To him, it was all simply a test that needed to be completed by the end of time.

"Where does it end?" I asked.

"Where it began," the Black Knight answered as he stopped to survey the mountains of the Slieve Mish that lay before us. "As the dream unfolds, the future is revealed."

***

The Slieve Mish mountains had always been considered a magical place by the Irish, pagan and Christian alike. It was here, in the cold mists of the Southwest that the ancient Druids had preserved the oldest ceremonies, maintaining their connections to the magical Tuatha de Danaan. In fact the name itself translated as the "slit where Time meets Space."

We were riding into that slit now, up the lonely mountain pass to where the air grew cold and the mist descended. As the Black Knight stopped at a cabin by the side of an icy glen, I knew the answer that had haunted me in my dreams was drawing near.

"We rest here, 'till morning," the Black Knight said as we tied up the horses.

Inside, I collapsed before the fire, stretching my legs out to its warmth. "Where are we?" I asked, as the Black Knight chose a spot in the darkened corner and removed his sword belt.

"The crossroads between then and now," he answered staring into the fire.

Now, ragged from my time in the saddle, my body suddenly feeling old beyond its years, I stared into the burning glow of the fire absorbing all the pain and frustration of the fourteenth Earl.

"This feels like hell," I said as I found myself drifting off into an old, familiar dream, the dream of Jerusalem. Only this time, the sense of it was even more real, the images of the cave beneath the temple and the multi-colored eggs that lay within the egg, vibrant.

There was the glowing egg before me, open to the images of light, flowing out like an endless rain. There was the beautiful woman in the white dress, Siobhan, holding back the three black horses in one hand and the red gem in the other.

I saw it all as it unfolded before my eyes, felt the swirling power of the images and heard the voices call to me. I pulled myself from the trance and bolted up the stairs. I remembered now. I remembered all of it; the woman, Strongbow and the treachery, but most of all I remembered the promise I had made of protection. In return for the knowledge, I had promised to save them and now, nine-hundred years later, was my chance.

Fire leapt from the temple as I reached the main floor, the air thick with blinding smoke. I leapt over bodies heaped by the stairwell and climbed toward the screams.

Reaching the top of the stairs, I felt a cold chill come over me and as I turned the corner, realized that the deep, nauseous feeling could mean only one thing.

"Get out of my way!" I yelled as the Black Knight stood before me, blocking my path. "You've brought me here, now let me finish."

"If you are not strong enough to defeat me, I cannot let you pass," the Black Knight said, in that crushed glass voice I had come to know so well.

"Get out, you blackened son of a bitch!" I cursed as I threw myself into him only to find myself on the rooftop facing the veiled woman and her family as they bargained with Gilbert for their lives.

"This is not the past that I remember," I thought as I watched the woman's little mother handing over sacred parchments to Gilbert, parchments that diagramed the elaborate placement of the colored stones.

A rage filled me as I drew my knife and charged. Emerging like a phantom from the blinding smoke, I struck hard on Gilbert's back, driving down like an assassin.

But in the smoke and confusion my blade deflected and with a screech of steel, skidded into softer flesh.

The instant it occurred, I realized I had missed my mark, but as the smoke cleared I felt the horror of my mistake. Instead of the greedy alchemist, my knife had struck the veiled woman squarely between the ribs. And as she gasped for breath, the veil wrenched from her face, I realized that the woman I'd killed was my own Elizabeth, the same woman I'd married almost nine-hundred years later.

The past and the present were one in a matrix of connections, the memory of which could easily drive one to madness and I awoke screaming with the agony of the knowledge. But the dream wasn't over. God knew where I really was, but it wasn't tucked into some bed in a hotel on the outskirts of Dublin. I was still before the fire in the Slieve Mish cabin under the watchful eye of the Black Knight and as I drew a breath, I knew my mission was yet to be completed.

"It was me, it was always me." I whispered, realizing the full memory of myself in the past and the future. "I killed her."

"You paid for the red blood stone with the woman's life, with the fourteenth Earl's wife, Joan and the lives of all those you saw die today and yesterday and the day before. But their sacrifice is understood and accepted. Elizabeth gave you the red stone and with her blood she gave it life. And you would prove your loyalty by finding her in time and joining her again. The circle has been completed. The spiral nears its end."

"But why was I blind to it until now. Why this?" I asked as the fire dwindled.

"Would you have done this had you known what you had to do? Would you have done any of it?"

"Who could bear such sorrow," I asked as the first rays of dawn broke through the window.

"You," the Black Knight snapped back. "And that is why you chose to do it. But all of this is gone. Now, remember the past and the secrets it holds. Extract their meaning as you would the marrow from a bone and you will have your final answer."

The Black knight hissed and faded like a phantom, vaporizing into the shadows as he caught the rays of the rising sun.

Alone, without a guide in a ghostly land of myth and legend, I struggled painfully from the floor. I was an old man at fifty-two now and more than just my mind remembered the fourteenth and last Earl of Desmond. My body, with all its wounds, remembered him, too.

I remembered my entire dream, over four-hundred years of it. The last Earl of Desmond was the richest baron in Europe with an estate larger than any other nobleman. He'd had the pick of European elegance, a choice of princesses and queens for wives. But instead, he'd chosen Ireland as his bride, adopted ancient Celtic ways and customs and worn the cloak of Clan Geraldine instead. Geroid Mac Gerailt he'd come to call himself in his final days. But as I stepped alone from the cabin into the cold frost of that November 11th, 1583 I realized there was one more thing for me to learn.

"It's him." The gruff man with the scraggly beard yelled as he wrestled me to the ground.

"But why? Why like this?" I offered.

"Because the Queen is in need of your skull," the man said as he raised an old rusted sword then brought it down hard.

LONDON

Security was having a worse than usual night at Transitron. Malcolm, tucked down deep in his lab had even been asked to check with NASA on sun spot activity, the interference had been so violent. Right before dawn, it had almost seemed as if his equipment was going to jump right off the shelf. Some kind of interference was moving in across a broad band of frequencies, popping circuits left and right. But then as the sun rose over the eastern shore and shown brightly on the city of London, it suddenly stopped. The white-out interference had never cut out quite that abruptly before, nor had the period after been quite so quiet.

Now, as Malcolm fiddled with the dials and checked the entire spectrum on his waveform monitors, he understood the reason for the quietness. As he surveyed the blank screens, pulseless and blank, he realized there was no spectrum.

Alissa noticed it too as she awoke in her London apartment from a dream of her father galloping on his white mare across the sky.

"He knows. He really knows," she said to herself.

Lord Gilbert knew, too. Using his web of satellites, he'd programmed his computers with the latest technology to probe Paul's dream world for secrets and had been doing it for years.

Using the ancient ritual magic on Earl Gerald's captured skull which he'd inherited from his father, his surveillance of Paul's dreams had led him directly to the home of the Grail, Bru Oengusa. But somewhere south of Dublin it had broken down.

Due to the Black Knight, a huge surge of power had poured back through the system and while leaving Gilbert's electronics essentially intact, it had turned the skull to powder.

Now, the magic spells the Elizabethans had used to overcome the Geraldine dream four hundred years before, had been broken. Paul was finally freed to do what his ancestors had come all the way to Ireland to complete and for the first time in his life, Lord Gilbert was running blind to the future.

As he screamed into the phone with no more than a handful of dust as the Winter Solstice approached, he knew it was time to take desperate action.

"Get me the board of directors." He said frantically.

ABBEYFEALE IRELAND, DECEMBER 19

I awoke from a coma-like sleep, surrounded by dozens of my Irish cousins; men, women, children of all ages and one very, very old man, Great Uncle Ned. A young man with red hair and freckles, Devon was bending down over my heart to check my breathing. Then convinced I was, gave the thumbs up.

"He's alive. I think he's actually alive," he said to the cheering crowd, as he turned and smiled broadly.

I had somehow arrived at my family's farm, essentially intact not far from the very spot where the last Earl of Desmond had lost his head four hundred years before. According to the telling, I had arrived unconscious, strapped to the saddle of a black horse and as the sun streamed into my eyes, the long journey of over four hundred years all came back to me.

It was as if I'd awoken from a four hundred year dream, a long, intense and at times tragic dream of conquest and famine, hardship and at last—exile to America. The Elizabethans had vanquished the Fitzgerald family, expropriated their million acres of farmland and gone on to conquer the world.

Gerald's head had been dried and salted, then sent to Queen Elizabeth as a gift. She'd sat with it in closed chambers for an entire morning before gifting it to her court sorcerer and Cabalist, John Dee.

A remnant of the Geraldine clan had struggled to stay together and remained on the land despite its new owners.

What had been done to the native Irish by their invasion had now been done to them. Now, farming the same sacred land by the shores of Lough Gur that they'd once owned, the family grew again. Within a few hundred years they again became so prominent they had become the first family of Ireland and for a brief time, the first family of America.

But John Fitzgerald Kennedy's Grail Knighthood was consumed by the same divisions as had marked the Crusades, and his family's persistent alliance with Rome only guaranteed the Templars desire for revenge. Over nine hundred years, the feud that had begun over the conquest of Jerusalem had spread to the courts of Europe, the farmlands of Ireland and the Presidency of the United States. And whether he knew it or not John Fitzgerald Kennedy had been just another score to settle in a competition as old as the Grail itself.

That night, as I sat by the turf fire in the old stone house next to Ned's farm, I told and retold the strange tale to the children of the family and how I had mysteriously wound up at their doorstep on the back of a black horse.

"And with one swift clip of the sword they cut off my head and took it to Queen Elizabeth, where she sat with it all morning long. And there it's been sleeping, until the very day I awoke up here."

The children stared, red cheeked and wide eyed as they listened to my words.

"Tell us again about the Black Knights cousin Paul. Tell us about the Black Knights in the Temple of Solomon."

"Cousin Paul's had a very tiring trip and its time for you to go to bed," Devon said as he picked up two of the littlest and carried them up the stairs. "We'll all see cousin Paul in the morning and you can tell him about your dreams then."

"Goodnight, cousin Paul," the crowd of little ones echoed as they followed their father off to bed leaving me alone by the fire with my old and great uncle Ned.

Ned was as old as the land itself, my grandfather's brother, he'd farmed the land all his life under the northern sun. Now his eyes were as yellowed by cataracts as the high priest of the temple, but his message was clear. "Come closer by the fire and let me see Billy's boy," he whispered as he shifted his bent frame.

I pulled closer as the old man inspected my face like a watchmaker examining the works of an old timepiece.

"Your father never returned here."

"No," I replied, still feeling an acute sense of loss for my father thirty five years after his death. "He died when I was quite young."

"Pity." Ned sighed. "Eight-hundred and thirty-three years we've been on this land. First as conquerors then as the conquered. In the end, it's all the same. It's the land that counts. If you love her, she loves you back, whether you're rich or poor. I just wish your father had seen it."

Tears fell from my eyes as I thought about it. "Maybe he does, through me."

Ned paused a moment. "Were you there when he died?" He asked.

"Yes."

"And what did you see? Was there a dying wish, the sign of the cross?" Ned added as he blessed himself.

I tried to remember. "No. It was sudden. But now that I think about it . . . "

Ned looked on, anxious with anticipation.

"His legs were bent in this strange angle. You know, I remembered thinking at the time how odd it was that he should die with his legs crossed. But now that I think of it, it was the same pose as those knights in the Templar church I told you about."

"The Holy Knights who'd done service in Jerusalem. Only you didn't know about them at the time, did you?" He asked squinting in the firelight.

"No." I answered.

"Come with me," Ned said, as he took me by the arm, grabbed a gas lantern and led me through the door. "I've been waiting to tell somebody about this all my life and now the time has finally arrived."

I followed Ned closely as he walked the well worn steps of the farmhouse, down the narrow path to the family graveyard. Then as he bent down with great pain, he motioned for me to help him move a headstone to one side and as we did, he retrieved a small lead box.

"I found this in the floor of the new barn when I was just a boy," he said, prying the lid back and removing a smooth round red stone. "I took it home and stored it under my pillow. That night I saw things I'd never seen; such sights, such sounds, ladies in beautiful gowns, castles that seemed to glow like crystal. Horses and riders in silver and black carrying the white flag with the red cross."

Ned closed his eyes as he remembered. "Then I saw a lady, a beautiful blond lady standing in the clouds with three black horses. She was holding them back with her right hand. When I opened my eyes she was in my room. I could hardly believe it was happening. She told me that I should be the guardian of the stone and that I should never reveal it to anyone until one day a son of Desmond would come from the West."

Ned opened his eyes and handed me the stone. "I'm 102 years old tomorrow, Paul. I think I've waited long enough."

✳✳✳

Inside the boardroom at Transitron Lord Gilbert was running damage control.

"It's here. What we've spent 900 years waiting for has arrived. Do you see any difference? You still arose at the proper hour, drank your coffee and drove to work? No banshees wailing at you from darkened glens, no hordes of ghostly warriors pouring from the sky and into your porridge?" he said, staring out the window at the Millennium Wheel.

"But the electronics? Can the electronics sustain the marriage?" Lord De Burgo countered, containing an urge to panic.

"Long enough to get what we want from the old bitch Semiramis and get out. But we'll have to be quick. The electronics can be maintained only so long as I can project into the future and that image is growing dim. I need possession of one more stone if I'm to make our creation permanent and complete what we began in Jerusalem."

"My God. It's really happening." Lord Sidney squawked as he loosened his tie.

"Of course it's happening," Lord Gilbert shouted back, glaring at Sidney as he slumped into his chair. "Nine-hundred years ago, King William Rufus summoned our ancestors to Jerusalem to return the Grail of life to Britain. They didn't know where it would take them or what it would ask, but they followed it. Now, nine-hundred years later their vision of the future has arrived. In a matter of hours a huge wave of energy will wash over the earth, changing, forming and reshaping everything we know. Through our electronics we will control that change, modulate it and limit its effects."

"You're absolutely sure we can do this?" Lord Montgomery snarled. "You're sure we can maintain our physical bodies in a purified state supported entirely by electronics?"

Gilbert was insistent.

"It is the goal of our entire spiritual evolution, to shed this dead skin and assume a higher form. Traditionally this mass migration of souls was done by the chosen, through the sacred marriage, the Hieros Gamos. This time we will have a say in who the bridegroom will be."

Montgomery persisted. "But Queen Elizabeth, the Faerie Queen herself, chose Earl Gerald's dream as the host for the last four hundred years. What makes you so sure she'd choose us?"

A young assistant entered with a thick folder and laid it on the table before Lord Gilbert. "Here are the dossiers you asked for, your Lordship."

Gilbert flipped it open to a series of papers turning to a photograph of Paul and his family. "Because Paul has provided us with the appropriate Monad, his daughter Alissa."

LONDON, SOLSTICE EVE

The phone rang as Alissa tried to reassemble the bits of her broken apartment. It was Rick. Though she still harbored doubts about his motives, she found herself warming as she talked on the phone. "The police said the burglars left no evidence. As far as they're concerned. There is nothing they can do."

"And what about your father? Has there been any word?" Rick asked cautiously.

Alissa paused for a moment and bit her lip. She knew what her father thought of Rick. The idea of betraying his confidence to such a man sent chills down her spine. But something in his voice, some slender thread told her she had to break with the past and in a short moment, she confessed.

"He's with the family in Ireland."

"When do we leave?" Rick asked, before Alissa had time to reconsider.

"I'm not sure he's ready for that," Alissa moaned, self consciously.

But Rick was serious, intent on his purpose. "I think he'll have to be. There are things he needs to know about my boss Lord Gilbert, important things ... "

"Hold on Rick." Alissa said as the doorbell rang. "There's someone here."

"No Alissa. Don't go to the door." Rick said, too late to stop her from dropping the phone. "Alissa, Alissa, Alissa!"

Even though he'd been unable to put a finger on it, all day long, he'd had a feeling that something was wrong. As the long silence was followed by a short click, his worst fears seemed to come to pass. "Alissa."

***

On a narrow stretch of country road in Limerick, children ran from post to post, lighting the torches that would guide the guests to the celebration of the Winter Solstice, and celebrate Uncle Ned's one hundred and second birthday.

Fiddle music and Irish reels filled the still night air as the cars approached the canvas tent thrown up for the occasion. It was a party to match anything thrown at the Desmond castles of Crom Abu or Askeaton as the huge white building seemed to heave and sway.

"Did Alissa get out of London before the traffic?" Devon asked, as I watched Uncle Ned be led around the floor by a bevy of elderly—but available women.

"She should be here at any moment," I told him, watching my great uncle twist and twirl around the ladies like a man at least half his age. "At least that was the plan."

***

Not far away, a small black helicopter registered out of London to Transitron Ltd. sped towards Abbeyfeale. Sighting the large lighted tent, it hovered momentarily near the ruins of an old Desmond castle then settled slowly down in the center of a torch-lit, frozen field. Inside the tent, the noise of the rotor was barely noticed but as Rick Kendall entered the doorway, the strange invader instantly drew Paul's attention.

***

"My daughter had better be three feet behind you Kendall," I found myself shouting as I pushed through the center of the swirling crowd.

"She's not here?" Rick asked, as the crowd stopped and stared in our direction.

"No. And neither will you be in a minute."

The entire hall now seemed to circle around Rick, moving toward him like a swarm of bees.

"Then she's gone, Paul," Rick said, a strange defeated look on his face. "She's been taken as a hostage."

For years I'd built up a case against this man, a loathing born from the loss of my wife. Now he was telling me my daughter had been consumed as well. But after what I'd been through I now accepted it wasn't him. It was Gilbert. It had always been Gilbert and his jealousy.

"I should have expected it," I said taking a deep breath.

"How?" A dumbfounded Rick mumbled as he eyed the crowd of Fitzgeralds crowded around. "How could you have expected that Alissa would be abducted?"

"I'll explain on the way back to London."

***

Back inside the farmhouse, I stared into the bedroom mirror and waited. I knew the Black Knight should be lurking somewhere around, somewhere on the other side of the mirror watching, hoping for the opportunity to spring another surprise attack. But he was nowhere in sight. Perhaps his mission was complete. There was little choice but to finish the course now. The Black Knight had led me to the truth of my own existence, caused me to relive nine hundred years of experience and that experience had brought me back to the red stone that was the key to the Grail. I went to the bed and removed it from under the pillow, and as I did I could feel the changes that were already underway. Whatever reality was, it was different now than it had been before. If anything it seemed more like a dream, more open and fluid, waiting to be shaped by a new dreamer. Only now I was tired of the dreaming and wanted only to wake up.

***

The ride back to London was fast as the little black copter crossed the Irish Sea and headed inland. But it was slow enough for me to fill in the details of the nine-hundred year quest.

"Tell me. What the hell is happening?" Rick asked, now acting more like a student than a news executive.

"Its some kind of mass evolution that occurs at very specific intervals in history. Plato complained in the Timaeus that after such events, civilization had to start over again, that everything was ruined. But it was only ruined for those who hadn't learned the lessons of the previous twenty four thousand year cycle. For those that misunderstood the purpose of the material world, they were forced to come back and rebuild it from scratch to learn the lessons they'd missed the first time."

"Then what happened to the rest?"

"They walked through into some other dimension of consciousness, some higher dimension that vibrates at a different frequency than this one," I said. "Normally, we could only see it or hear it in our dreams, but as we pass into it consciously, it will become our new reality."

"And what does the stone do?" Rick asked.

"It brings us into it embodied, as it brought us here thousands of years ago. The Crusader Gerald was spiritually blinded by its serpent guardian retrieving it from Jerusalem. But as his family learned to live with its power, they gained the sight and the wisdom to use it. It was then my job to figure out what had begun in Jerusalem and restore the stone to its proper place at the appointed time."

Rick sat quietly, watching the lights of London approach from the East. "But how was Gilbert able to track you?"

"Necromancy. The last Earl of Desmond's skull provided him with a door into every Geraldine consciousness. The old incantations were preserved in the rituals taught to him by Bledri at Pembroke. He's been floating around in our dreams waiting for this time and place. He knew all along what we were supposed to do. He just waited for one of us to do it."

Rick shook his head. "Talk about a long term strategy. Then I guess Lord Gilbert will get what he wants."

"They've been dragging my family members to London and throwing them in the tower for the last 800 years. But they never got what they were looking for. He obviously can't manufacture the stone or he'd never have taken the risks with both me and Alissa."

I removed the stone from my pocket and showed it to Rick. "This one is obviously the key, the one that fills the body of creation with the blood of life and keeps it alive. It's the heart of the whole dimension. Without it, Gilbert's electronics are just smoke and mirrors."

Rick shook his head in disbelief as the huge Millennium Wheel approached from the distance. "So what will he do next?"

* * *

Lord Gilbert joined his board as they stared into the soundproof "environment room" in the basement of Transitron. "How's the girl? He said as he observed a happy child-like Alissa interacting with holograms of her mother and father at a carnival.

"Completely immersed," De Burgo answered comparing a video monitor with the simple holographic environment he saw before him. "It's amazing. Her mind's filling in all the details."

"In a few hours she'll be filling out the details in our new world." Gilbert said, coldly.

De Burgo was still troubled. "But how do we get her out to the Millennium Wheel?"

"She'll do anything as long as she thinks I'm Paul," Gilbert answered. "And that's what we want her to think."

"Then we'll have to keep her away from the real one," De Burgo added cynically. "Won't we?"

A guard, dressed in black and toting electronic gear, emerged from a nearby room. "Satellite just picked them up, Lord Gilbert. They'll be here soon."

Gilbert threw back his head, causing his long red hair to fly. "I know. I can feel him. It's been so long," he said as he swung his head around in a slow spiral then snapped it forward, twisting it like some circus freak. "Tell security to buzz him through. I've waited a long time for this."

The antennas on the Transitron building jabbed the night sky like brilliant hypodermic needles as the helicopter approached, search lights probing the sky.

"We'll go in from the roof," Rick said as he surveyed the building. There's a helipad there."

"I'll go in alone," I said.

"No." Rick shot back. "I can protect you."

I couldn't contain the smile as I recalled the dream of Jerusalem. "I've had more experience with this guy than you can imagine. Besides, my time is up. I have nothing left to do but this."

"Then what can I do?" Rick asked, as he looked at me eagerly.

I quietly took the red stone from my pocket as I whispered a destination into Rick's ear. "I'll meet you there when I'm done," I said, dropping it into Rick's pocket as the skids of the small helicopter touched down atop the pad.

"Take the stairs down one flight. There's an elevator there that will take you to the sub-basement," Rick yelled toward me as I stepped from the craft and walked toward the doors.

IN HELD
TWAS IN I

A loud hum filled the corridor as I approached the elevator, a hum not unlike that day in the Templar Cathedral. It almost made me dizzy as it vibrated through me, resonating at a frequency that was clearly overpowering.

I took a deep breath and pushed the button, then stared into the void as the doors opened. I was descending into Gilbert's world like Parcival descending into the dark forest. I hoped I was ready for the final test.

***

Rick yelled to the pilot as he swung the helicopter into the London sky, then circled the building. "Put me down in that parking lot next door."

The pilot looked at Rick suspiciously but did as he was told, finding an opening on the three story garage roof and zipping down for a landing.

"Happy Solstice!" Rick said as he paused at the copter door then hurried to his car.

"Ya, right," the black suited pilot sneered back as he flipped a set of switches on his console, causing a small red blip to blink on his radar screen.

"Home. This is Night Stalker. Target is sending. What now?"

"Keep on him." The voice on the radio replied. "Just make sure he doesn't notice."

"Who's going to notice?" The pilot replied, pulling back on the throttle and zipping up into the sky.

***

The building continued to pulse as I descended down the long thin glass tube into the core of the Transitron building. It was startling to see the huge Cray computers and Thinking Machines—cranking out complex algorithms—now that I knew what they were to be used for. Who were they thinking about, I wondered as the elevator came to a stop. What reality were they projecting on an unsuspecting populace?

I didn't have long to wait as the elevator doors opened and I stood facing a grinning Lord Gilbert.

"So, you've arrived on schedule," Gilbert said, as he held out a hand in welcome. "Now the millennium wheel can finally fulfill it function."

Gilbert draped a long arm around my shoulder, then led me through the cavernous underground hold of Transitron, filled to the heights with pulsing electrical switch boxes and circuit frames.

"I think we should have gotten together sooner though, don't you?"

"Your technology is very impressive, Lord Gilbert . . ." I said, as the hum seemed to groan louder ". . . .or would you prefer Strongbow?"

Gilbert smiled.

"It's nice of you to remember. Longevity is one of the benefits of alchemy. What you see here is the largest bank of computing power in the world. From this substation I control nearly every computer on the planet."

"That's quite an accomplishment."

"Maintaining the structure of this dimension, it's shape and form, its memory is no easy task." Gilbert said, gloating. "We came on line in just the nick of TIME."

"Which is what I assume you now control." I surmised.

"Clever and insightful. Ten thousand years of history—life and death—coded—copyrighted and installed in the silicon brain of Transitron. Galileo move over. We are the new universe."

"And what do you think people will do when they wake up to find they've become part of your circuitry."

Gilbert scrunched up his forehead as if confounded. "Thank me, of course. You really think people will miss reincarnating into this shit-hole of an existence. People have been trying to get off this wheel of life since Adam. Now they can come ride on my wheel."

"So that's what you really built it for."

"And it will be that way forever. That is with the help of the missing stone." Gilbert said playfully.

"With all your electronics, you still need some 3 million year old red rock to make it work?" I offered, pausing to stare at the huge banks of black computers, clicking and blinking.

"There are just some things even I can't do better than God. Now if you'd please, hand it over." Gilbert said, smiling.

"Not without my daughter."

Gilbert feigned innocence, badly. "Did someone say I had your daughter?"

"Cut the bullshit Strongbow."

Gilbert grew enraged. "Bullshit. I'll tell you what Bullshit is. Bullshit is a King granting the lowly constable of one of his castles a Grail princess when I 'm already running the show. Now take it from me, that's bullshit."

"That was 900 years ago."

"As far as I'm concerned it happened yesterday. Nobody steals a Grail princess right out of my own Earldom and gets away with it, nobody, not even a King. And I think it's about time I made up for the insult." He said.

There was little I could do but glare. "And you believe my daughter can do that for you?"

"You understand the ancient ways Paul, the sacrifices and the offerings. After all that I've suffered I'm entitled to the first fruits. Besides. You're in no position to bargain. Give me what should rightfully have been mine and I'll consider returning your daughter. Give me the stone."

"I don't have it."

Gilbert growled. "Then you'd better get it because time is running out. In a little over an hour, a cosmic wave that's been cycling its way towards us for twenty-four thousand years is going to start resonating over this planet and as dawn breaks the sun's rays will start changing that wave to particles. Do you know what that means?" Unless a new form is there to take the old one's place everything is washed away, reality itself. And not just any form will do. Your daughter is very special that way."

"But you've been preparing for a thousand years. How can you not be ready?"

Gilbert turned away, a look of genuine fear in his eyes.

"There is no way to know. All the ancient books from the Sumerian to the Akkadian to the Mayan call for the world to end now, that this dimension of experience will cease to exist. But nobody really knows what that means. Imagine the last thousand years of history wiped out as it courses through. Every molecule, every fiber vibrated and shattered to pieces as it rips through the entire fabric of the planet, through the entire fabric of us."

"You can't stop it, Lord Gilbert." I said, looking around at all the furious, blinking machines.

"I can and I will." Gilbert whispered. "And you're going to help me."

∗∗∗

On the other side of town, Rick slowed, checking the rear view mirror as he approached the East Street Stables. It was quiet, so quiet he confidently left the car and walked to the side door.

But high above, the little black helicopter observed his every move, and as he entered the building, the pilot took action. "Night Stalker to all units. Move in."

Inside, the old grey haired attendant led Rick down the long central corridor of the barn to the stall of Paul's white mare.

"Here's Juno," he said as he unlatched the gate and ushered Rick inside. "Beautiful old girl she is, too."

The mare cast a huge brown eye on the stranger, sizing him up as the attendant turned and headed back to his desk.

"Whoa girl, whoa," Rick said as he patted Juno on the neck. Paul sent me to say hello." She whinnied as he leaned over and whispered in her ear. "He also sent me here to hide this."

Rick pulled out the stone and stared at it as the horse reared back on her hind legs. It was strange how she seemed to understand, Rick thought and even stranger how she reacted as she immediately stamped her hoof on a loose wooden floor board, indicating something was underneath.

"She does know what I'm saying," he mumbled as he pulled away the loose board and reached inside, fishing around until he came upon a package. "I'll be a son of a gun," he said out loud as he pulled a brown manila envelope wrapped in plastic from the hole and held it to the light. "It's Paul's missing manuscript."

✳✳✳

Outside, a swat team, dressed in black military fatigues silently approached the building as the black helicopter hovered overhead. They were quiet, as quiet and solemn as any holy warriors as they crept up to the barn and burst through the doors. Their mission was simple. Find the stone and return with it, no matter what the cost.

Rick barely even heard them as they approached. But as the lights died and the horses screamed the first thing he tried to do was hide it.

✳✳✳

Inside Transitron, Paul and Lord Gilbert finalized their bargaining session.

"What did you mean by saying my daughter was special to this process?" I asked, watching the blinking lights reflect off Gilbert's eyes.

"Your daughter is our Monad, a true Grail Monad. You didn't think Rufus allowed himself to be shot that day 900 years ago without knowing the downstream benefits. Rufus committed Gerald to a mission. He'd studied the books, the mathematics, the cycles of moon and sun. He knew how long it would take to create a new form to achieve spiritual perfection. Marrying him off to a brood mare like Nest guaranteed an entire race would be available when the time came, as long as someone was left who knew what the seed was planted for." Gilbert said, the strain finally showing on his face. "And I am that someone."

"Alissa won't be your new Monad, Gilbert. She's too smart to work for someone like you."

"She doesn't have a choice and neither do you. Time is running out, tick, tick, tick. Meet me at the millennium wheel in one hour or you'll never see your daughter again, not even in your dreams."

***

The dark London streets were empty as Lord Gilbert's cameras surveilled Paul make his way to a cab.

"I want the city put under lock and key," the huge man said as an assistant emerged from the shadows and whispered in his ear. "And alert the army that two IRA bombers have entered the city and are headed for the Wheel. They are to be apprehended. And be quick about it. There isn't much time."

"Yes Sir," the assistant barked back with military precision.

***

Military vehicles swept into action and took up positions on deserted street corners as the cab sped towards Hyde Park. By the time the car approached the sign that read, "East Street Stables" the perimeter of the city was surrounded in an iron ring.

"Hold it," I told the cabby as I surveyed the darkened building from the back seat of the cab. "There's supposed to be a watchman there twenty-four hours a day."

Outside the air had suddenly turned balmy, a silvery mist floated on the breeze. It tingled as I stepped into it.

I ordered the cabby to wait and walked to the side door. Inside, the place was a shambles—the watchman slumped over his desk. As I ran towards Juno's stall—I saw Rick sprawled on the floor.

"They have the stone," he said as I helped him to his feet. "But they didn't get this."

Rick swayed as he pulled the manila envelope containing my manuscript from his jacket.

"Hold on to it," I told him, trying to steady him on his feet. "We have less than an hour."

The stable was turning to a madhouse now as horses, sensing the changing vibrations, pounded their hooves against the doors and walls trying to escape.

"Can you make it?" I asked as I lifted Rick up under the shoulder.

Rick grunted painfully. "I guess," he said as we staggered toward the door.

Outside the night was growing stranger, the silvery mist now filling the air. I could feel the sensations, like waves of mild electric current running through me.

"It's what Gilbert feared would happen" Rick said, as we reached the cab. "The electronics can't hold the dimension together alone without the red stone. The signals have to be balanced exactly or else the dimensional walls break apart."

Inside the cab, the driver seemed disoriented, and as he fiddled with the radio the silvery mist seemed to congeal around him and surround him in the sound. "I don't understand," he said switching the dial around the spectrum. "No matter what I tune in I get the same music."

"Gilbert's probably cranked up the juice to compensate for the breakdown. If he doesn't get that stone into place soon, the whole thing is gonna' blow." Rick said.

All over London a great sigh could be heard as Transitron's power surge of electromagnetic waves blanketed the city causing the silvery mist to coalesce into a thousand various forms.

I could see them now as semi-transparent beings as wave after shimmering wave moved in, washing through the trees and engulfing the cab as it swept across the road.

"Damn!" The driver said as the ignition switch emitted a high pitched whine and the battery died. "It's these electronic ignitions. Blasted things."

"It's more than that." I said as a the entire car seemed to flicker and pulse, as if each molecule of its makeup was being rearranged into a new configuration. "If what I heard tonight is true, you're about to witness something you've never seen or heard before."

The dimensional walls of this reality were breaking down right before our eyes. All over London, stop lights blinked then flickered and died as old analog circuits unprepared for the blanket surge, shorted out then disappeared as they were drawn into another dimension. Store windows cracked as TV sets and radios emitted the same high pitched scream, some melting down while others came to life with three dimensional characters stepping out from the screens as hologram-like ghosts. Music played, bands marched from out of nowhere, down the street and back to nowhere as the air shimmered and glowed.

Everything was being pulsed at higher and higher frequencies, discordant harmonies splitting wires and exploding transformers. Were it not for Transitron's powerful signal the entire dimension of reality would have disappeared.

"What'll we do?" Rick said, staring at his analogue watch, which now jumped erratically backwards and forwards in time. "We'll never get there in time. There is no time."

Two Saracen armored cars sped from each direction down the street then screeched to a halt fifty yards from the barn. I could hear soldiers voices in the distance and as they approached, I wondered for the first time after nine-hundred years whether I was about to fail.

"Looks like we may never make it. Nothing's going to work in this." Rick complained, echoing my thoughts.

"The horses in the barn are still working" I told him, giving the gash on his head a quick look over. "If you're O.K. we'll use them."

"I'll do," Rick said, as we bolted back into the barn.

I snatched a bridle from the wall and headed down toward Juno. "There's no time for a saddle," I said. Grab one of these and come with me."

"I'm sorry Paul," Rick groaned as he followed me down the aisle past the horses. "I couldn't have imagined any of this."

For the first time in my memory Rick's sincerity moved me. "How could you? How could anybody? The whole point has been to cut us off from the past so we don't know who we are."

"And that made it easy for Gilbert to get away with it," Rick admitted as I fastened the bridle onto my horse.

"He hasn't got away with it yet," I said, as I mounted Juno and led her from the stall. "C'mon!"

"I don't ride," Rick stammered.

"Then just hold on," I said, as I extended a hand and pulled him up behind me.

I led the white mare past the other stalls, opening them as we went, then led the panicked horses into the aisle and up to the door.

"What do we do now?" Rick asked as the horses bolted and kicked in the crowded quarters, jammed in at the end of the barn.

"We pray." I said, realizing the situation was just as hopeless as it could be. But my prayer seemed to have a calming effect on the horses and as I heard the distinct rhythm of clicking hooves from the darkness at the distant end of the barn, I knew that it had been answered.

"Who is that?" Rick asked as he squinted into the dark.

"An old friend." I answered, as the Black Knight, replete in his threatening dull black armor emerged, riding Alissa's black stallion, Attila.

Rick hooted in amazement as the Black Knight pushed his way through the skittish horses and turned my way, offering me a steely smile—then reared back on the black stallion and kicked the large double door from its hinges.

Outside, the soldiers took up positions behind the Saracens and prepared their attack. But the raging assault by the Black Knight took them completely by surprise. By the time we burst from the barn and vaulted the Saracens, the frightened soldiers could do little but stare in bewilderment and as we disappeared into the night, we made our escape.

***

In the park outside the Millennium Wheel, Gilbert's party gathered for the main event. Dressed in medieval armor to commemorate their ancestors' service in the Crusades they assembled into two columns and raised swords as Lord Gilbert marched Alissa toward the Millennium Wheel, the red stone clutched tightly in is hand.

"Are we're going on the wheel again, Dad?" Alissa said as they approached the brightly lit wheel.

"Yes, Alissa," Gilbert said, opening the door to one of the sixty cabins. "You liked it so much the first time, we're going to go around again."

Gilbert's board members peeled off and circled to face each other, then knelt on one knee as a huge electromagnetic wave seemed to form around the wheel.

"The wheel works." De Burgo said, as his eyes scanned the bright multi-colored waves of energy pulsing and contracting through the sky like some enormous jelly fish.

Lightning and thunder struck in the distance as Gilbert gazed up at the formation, growing stronger and stronger in the night sky.

"It works," he whispered holding the stone up to the light and closing his eyes. "Now the dream will be mine."

***

I could see the spectacle like a huge aurora from the other side of the river as two Saracens picked up our trail and followed in hot pursuit.

"How come the taxi won't go and they will?" Rick said, holding on for dear life as we zig-zagged across an open field.

"They must be shielded for EMP, Electro Magnetic Pulse," I said as Juno darted under a helicopter and headed for the trees.

As Lord Gilbert had carefully planned, his electronics were working—focusing and redirecting the waves into a vortex created by his wheel then redirecting that energy into his artificial electronic web as it fanned out across the globe.

The effect was to maintain the illusion of existence just the way it had always been. But soon, the real test would come, as the first rays of the Solstice sun threatened to turn wave into matter as they had thousands of years ago at Bru Oengusa.

It had ultimately been the purpose of the Hieros Gamos, the sacred marriage to prepare the earth and its inhabitants for this passage to a new dimension. But over the millennia that purpose had been lost. Removed from their natural role in the process, the sleeping population had no understanding of what was now occurring. And as they awakened and climbed from their beds, they found themselves confronted by a surrealistic nightmare of Biblical proportions.

"Look at the sky!" People screamed as phantom images from the past poured from the darkened skies and were drawn to the Millennium Wheel, protected now by the only secure power supply in the city. "It's Ezekiel's wheel. This is the judgement!"

***

We escaped through the trees, emerging onto an abandoned industrial site down by the river. But as we explored a way across, we found ourselves blocked at every turn.

"Can your horse swim?" Rick asked as we galloped up and down the river bank now beginning to swell with people.

"They'd shoot us before we got across or pick us up on the other side," I said.

"Then we might as well throw in the towel." Rick said, throwing up his hands and scanning the glowing wheel on the other side of the river. "Look at that thing. It's just the way he planned, focusing the signal, structuring it for his computers so he can send it over the globe. Jesus! It was right in front of me the whole time."

"It's no different than Bru Oengusa or Solomon's Temple. It's just newer. Our ancestors knew all about this stuff and they've been trying to warn us in our dreams."

***

A few hundred yards away on the other side of the river, Gilbert was ready for the dawn.

"Full power!" He called to his friends.

The wheel shook as it gained speed, then began to accelerate until the wave arced and flowed around it, bubbling and roiling, coursing through every molecule on the planet. To Gilbert it was just what he'd been waiting for and as the energy fields rattled and snapped around him, he clutched the red stone tightly and prepared to focus its energy.

***

I scanned the horizon over the heads of the multitude which seemed to grow by the minute. It seemed hopeless. The scene across the water was a truly miraculous sight as multi-colored fields of energy waxed and waned in the morning twilight. But it was not a miracle for me. It was a miracle for Lord Gilbert. I had followed my dreams from Afghanistan to London and right up to the edge of time. But at the last moment in that time, I found myself a river away from the role my life was intended to fill.

"What is it?" I asked, thinking Rick had tugged on my pant leg.

"I said nothing," Rick said, his eyes glazed over from the sight only a few hundred yards away.

I saw nothing either. But in a moment a tiny hand reached up from below and gently took the reigns. "It's Juicy John," I said as the crowd parted, miraculously revealing a hidden London Underground station.

"I'm dreaming," Rick said as he caught sight of a smiling Juicy John Pink standing at the top of the stairs, Juno's reigns clutched tightly in his hand.

"Keep it up. It's working."

***

Back inside Lord Gilbert's cabin, the illusory images of a childhood carnival that flooded Alissa's mind were beginning to flicker and as Paul drew nearer from under the Thames, Gilbert's face began to lose the appearance of her father.

"Dad. What's the matter with your face?" She said trying to pull herself from the induced hologram.

"Nothing Alissa. Nothing." Gilbert said, grabbing the controls of the little Dream Catcher device as he tried to cover himself up.

But the shock waves from the pulsing waves rocked the car and as Gilbert fumbled to regain control he dropped the device. Immediately, Alissa's projected reality folded like a tent and she awoke from the trance, screaming.

No longer governed by the electronic illusion, Alissa's real consciousness altered the color of the flow, broadening it and giving it a new focus. Soon, the familiar images of reality that Gilbert had been maintaining began to disappear and in their place new shapes began to appear.

Angels, demons, gods and goddesses suddenly appeared. Where London's skyscrapers had been, castles materialized with ladies in grand dresses and knights in shining armor. But as this new world of images seemed to shimmer and glow, Lord Gilbert shrunk in fear to the bottom of the car. And as the power swirled and danced around the cabin, a clap of thunder broke and an ancient voice called out.

"We are the children of the Goddess Danaan and we have come to claim what is rightfully ours."

Suddenly, the green park surrounding the wheel was filled with the hum of Celtic warriors, their horses and war chariots galloping out of a widening crack in the dimension. Voices filled the cabin as images swirled around Gilbert, terrifying him as they flashed their swords and sang their war cries: "Aboo, Aboo, Aboo, Aboo!"

Back on the ground, Gilbert's benighted friends ran for cover, just as they had that night in Ossary eight-hundred years before, in 1170. Some screamed in panic, others cut and swiped with their swords at the warriors that swirled around the framework of the Millennium Wheel, but with little effect.

The men fled for protection toward the phalanx of British soldiers who fired into the air at the great, ghostly horde, but the bullets only disappeared, vanishing as the new dimension washed over them, then consumed the soldiers as well.

***

Inside the abandoned subway tunnel, Rick and I came to a stairwell and as we prepared to ascend, turned to Juicy John Pink to hear his farewell.

> "The Grail is here.
> It waits for you.
> It will not serve that you are two.
> But if your heart can find the way,
> It will lead the other to a brighter day."

Juicy John Pink smiled as he waved goodbye. As I spurred my horse up the stairs, he turned and headed back into the dark.

The green park surrounding the wheel was in chaos now, swords and guns, bits of medieval armor thrown down as we calmly approached the wheel and waited for Gilbert's cabin to slow. In seconds it came to a stop and he burst from the car, his knife in one hand, Alissa in the other. Beleaguered and besieged he stumbled to his knees as two phantom warriors appeared from behind, whacked him on the head and sped off.

"Aren't you a little old for carnival rides?" I asked as Gilbert tried to compose himself.

"This is no carnival ride, you bloody assassin. This is the prophecy of Daniel come to life on the banks of the Thames. The stone Kingdom will consume all kingdoms that ever were." Gilbert shook Alissa, her wrist clenched tightly in his huge fist. "And this is the means by which it works."

"The stone won't work for you, Gilbert," I said scornfully.

"And why not?"

"Because you weren't the one who was chosen to use it. I already told you that. It was signed in blood by Rufus on the celebration of Lugh on August 2, 1100 and it can't be undone."

Gilbert's face grew red as he pushed toward me. "I have the stone, and the secrets of holography. That's all I need to hold the Grail."

"But you took them. You violated the basic tenets of the Hieros Gamos. Don't you remember Brigit's test? Don't you know anything about the Grail?" I said as Gilbert flew into a rage.

"Grail? GRAIL? I built an empire that spans the entire planet. I pioneered electronics and computers that puts your puny brain to shame. I've engineered genetics that merge the worlds of human and machine. Don't tell me I'm not worthy of the Grail!"

"Then why can't you get it to work?" I said calmly, as a half dozen phantom warriors surrounded Gilbert.

Gilbert rose up, a powerful jealousy in his eyes.

"Because of you. Don't you remember how Nest laughed at me. How you always beat me to the punch. You were always the chosen, always the first," he said, raising his knife to Alissa's throat. "And now it's my turn to beat you."

"No." I said, dismounting from Juno. "Take me instead. You had Earl Gerald's head for four-hundred years to dream with. You can have mine now."

A light seemed to dawn in Gilbert's brain and for a moment he loosened his grip on Alissa's arm.

"Don't do it, Paul," Rick said. "You don't want to live in his dream anymore. Nobody should."

"And you'll make all this go away . . . " Gilbert said looking around at the scenery as it warped and morphed into hundreds of shapes and colors, ghosts and dragons appearing and disappearing at will. " . . . all this static?"

"You'll make it go away yourself. You'll have the power." I said, pointing to his head. "The real power."

"All right. If that's what it takes." Gilbert boasted, motioning me into the empty cabin. "Get in."

I paused for a moment, taking one last long look at Alissa, kissed her goodbye then entered as Gilbert quickly followed.

"Take her!" He said as he pushed Alissa away and slammed the door behind him.

Rick dismounted and took Alissa in his arms.

"We have to do something." Alissa said.

"Do what?" Rick said staring around at the Celtic warriors. "This is all a little over my head."

Bonfires were lit now on both sides of the Thames and people held torches to the sky as the phantoms cruised overhead, circled and swooped down on the gathering crowds. People ran through the streets screaming as they were pursued by their own ghosts or embraced and carried away by angels. But as the soldiers fled and the spirits moved out among the people the scene turned peaceful. One by one the shouts of joy could be heard as people recognized the images of their fathers and mothers, sons and daughters long since passed beyond the grave.

The commingling of the living and the dead was a strange sight to see as the two worlds of spirit and flesh were suddenly one. It was a day of judgement, but not the way it had been predicted, as tears turned to joy and the past was reunited with the present before the wheel of life.

Inside the cabin, Gilbert was excited as well.

"All right. What's next?" He asked as the Solstice Sun rose on the horizon, turning the silvery mist to gold with a sparking and hissing sound.

"Give me the stone," I said.

"Why?" Gilbert asked, with a look of horror on his face.

"Because I'm the one who has to hold it," I said, calmly. "The electronics won't contain it. The wave is too big. The new paradigms are in my head. If you want it to materialize a new world, it's got to go through me."

Gilbert paused, then reached into his pocket and pulled out the dull, lifeless red stone. Then as he stared at it longingly, he handed it to me.

In an instant it seemed to warm to my touch, giving off a glow that grew brighter by the second. Then, as the wave seemed to focus and channel into the cabin, the Millennium Wheel began to spin.

"I don't believe he's doing it for him," Alissa said, as the two watched the wheel trace into the sky, slowly at first, then faster until it carved a huge golden arc, with the red gem-like stone glowing from the center.

Inside, Gilbert was ecstatic, bubbling almost giddily as the world streaked by outside. "Now it works. The wheel actually works the way I planned. I knew it would. I knew if I designed it right it would ride on the wave, like Noah's Ark. I knew my father's reading of the ancient theories was correct. Matter and energy formed by conscious thought to make energy real, to congeal life forms."

Gilbert was caught up in the theories now, as the waves washed over him.

"I can feel it. No, better. I can see it. I can see it Paul, a new world where thought and creation are one. With this I have the power of the new God, control over all the frequencies, high and low. Think of it. All the way from the first Crusade to here, and I'm the winner. I am the new Great Organizing Dynamic."

He turned to me, green with envy. "I am G O D. Get it? Now, give me the stone."

Gilbert drew his dagger and lunged.

Outside, as Alissa and Rick watched the crowd slowly disappeared, the shapes and forms of the old world disappearing with them, dissolving into the sunlight like melting ice crystals. The wheel itself seemed a blur, a fiery red swirl of energy that seemed to emanate harmonious tones—a whisper at first, then louder as it spiraled outward.

"DomineoVeniteoSacramentumEoDeo."

Inside the cabin Gilbert was gaining the advantage, but as he freed his hand and raised his knife to strike again, the familiar sound of crushing glass filled the air. And as Gilbert turned, I witnessed his horror as he found himself wrapped in the vice-like grip of a mailed, black leather glove.

"Don't you love me the best?" The voice said, as Gilbert turned to see the face of the Black Knight staring back at him.

✳✳✳

A loud scream could be heard as the wheel began to slow and the great flood of energy began to settle into new vibrant forms, shimmering in the morning sunlight. It was like something from a dream. Unleashed spirits now drew back from where they had come, forming miles and miles of ribbon-like processions through the sky as angelic harmonies seemed to lift them and carry them off into new dimensions of light.

Tears rolled down Rick and Alissa's face as the sky brightened. Even Juno seemed changed. Drawn by the remaining swirls of light, she nuzzled Alissa, then charged off on a light bridge into an expanding dimension.

"She's gone." Alissa cried, turning to Rick.

Spinning itself to a stop, the wheel finally wound its way to where it had begun and as the door squeaked open, Rick and Alissa's eyes opened wide.

"Lord Gilbert?" Rick said as Gilbert emerged from the cabin, on his face a calm and gentle expression.

"Lord? I should be so lucky," he said, genuinely surprised.

Rick was baffled. "You're not Lord Gilbert, managing director of Transitron Communications?"

"Transitron? Funny you'd know about that," he said waving his hands, "That was just a dream I had a long time ago. I don't recall telling anyone about it. I run the wheel—that is, I take people where they want to go."

"Where's my father?" Alissa demanded, staring into the empty car. "What did you do with him?

"Your father?" Gilbert asked. "That man in the cabin? He's gone home. He didn't want to dream anymore."

"Then where can I find him?"

"He said to tell you it's all in the book."

Alissa turned to see a changed landscape as the sun rose over a newly glistening London, no sign of soldiers or police. "Where are we?" She said.

"Lugdunum, the stronghold of Lugh, god of light. Though you probably know it as London." Gilbert said.

"The River looks the same." Rick answered peering back down over the hill. "But its brighter, almost opal. The bridges and the buildings are different too. I'd say a completely different kind of architecture. It looks..," he said pausing as the implications registered. ". . . kind of like a painting in the Museum. Let's go down and see."

Together, the two walked down into the city, each amazed at the strange new environment and as they asked about the city they'd known most of their lives, they were greeted with stares and wonderment.

"Could you tell me how to get to the British Museum?" Alissa asked a passing woman.

"Museum?" The woman replied, genuinely confused by the question.

"The place where things from the past are kept." Alissa explained.

"This is a land where there is no past," she said, sensing Alissa's distress. "All time is now. But there is a memorial to the mind that created it. It's over there."

Rick and Alissa walked to the circular quartz monument that stood in the city center and read the inscription.

"In honor of Lugh, the Dagda and his son Angus, whose dream of time spanned the universe. May his thoughts live in our minds and his deeds in our hearts for all eternity. And may his brightness never cease."

The pair stared around them, bewildered at their new surroundings. Then as they lifted their eyes to the model of Bru Oengusa they let out a simultaneous sigh.

"He found it. He found the Grail and stepped through to the other side." Alissa said, tears welling from her eyes at the realization of what had occurred. She turned to Rick and smiled sadly. "We're not going to find him here."

In a nearby park, children danced hand in hand, playing a circle game. And as they sang a tune in an unfamiliar language, Rick withdrew the manuscript for Paul's new book from his jacket and began to read aloud.

"In a land beyond time, somewhere in the Irish countryside a man resembling Paul lay on a grassy hillside on a sunny day below a huge quartz monument. Below in the valley, games are being played and the carefree sound of children's voices can be heard. Then suddenly, a woman's voice is heard to call."

"Angus. The children have come for you to play."

The man squinted in the sunlight as he was suddenly surrounded by a dozen laughing children. Now dressed in the white robe of his father, the Dagda, he is joined by a young blond woman by the name of Siobhan, whose white dress blows in the mild breeze.

"Were you dreaming again?" She asked, kneeling by his side, filling the air with the smell of fresh wildflowers.

"Yes. I was dreaming a terrible dream, that the world was about to end and all this was about to disappear."

The woman laughed. "And did you save it then?"

Angus smiled and pulled the smallest child to his chest and hugged him. "Of course. That's what dreams are for."

Together, Angus, his father the Dagda and his family descended into the lush green valley and joined with the others in a great celebration of light and renewal.

That night before the bonfire as they presided over a great feast, the woman Siobhan and the man named Angus shared a toast and pledged to each other a love that would never die.

Author's Notes

DAGDA

It wasn't until I picked up the well known book written by Joseph Cambell on Occidental Mythology, The Masks of God, that the all the pieces finally fell into place."By various schools of modern scholarship," it read, "the Grail has been identified with the Dagda's caldron of plenty, the begging bowl of the Buddha in which four bowls, from four quarters were united, the Kaaba of the Great Mosque of Mecca, and the ultimate talismanic symbol of some sort of Gnostic-Manichaean rite of spiritual initiation, practiced possibly by the Knights Templar."

What made this statement so enlightening at that moment came as a result of a recent trip to Ireland and to the ancient "passage grave" of New Grange—also known by its Gaelic name as Bru Oengusa, or the Mansion of Angus, son of the Dagda.

To say the least, the neary six thousand year old Bru Oengusa is of mind-boggling construction and it was said that whoever the Dagda was, he had designed and built the so-called "passage-grave" for himself.

Originally built in the shape of an egg, its exterior facade is covered in an eleven foot wall of quartz crystal that glows in the early morning sun like some ancient solar time piece and in fact, at the winter solstice it receives the morning sun into its deepest interior. Older than the Temples of Mycenae and the Pyramids, wealthy Romans of the early Christian era had made pilgimages to it from Britain and left precious offerings of gold and jewelry to propitiate the spirits of its powerful gods, the Tuatha de Danann, or People of the Goddess Danu.

But like the Pyramids, which appear to have had some ceremonial function in addition to their role as tombs, what did this place do and why, over all other worldly sacred sites did Joseph Campbell consider it to be the home of the most sought after of relics, the Grail?

On the shortest day of the year a seventeen centimeter shaft of light impregnates the darkness of Bru Oengusa for exactly seventeen minutes, focusing an intense, almost laser-like light into the deepest cavity within.

As a seasonal time piece, Bru Oengusa still maintains this accuracy to the second. But laying sealed and virtually undisturbed for the more than five-thousand years of its life precludes the idea that it functioned as some ancient observatory to mark this date.

It would seem this geo-solar time machine served some other purpose for its creators, whose spiral and diamond-shaped carvings speak with a language of symbols that nearly five-thousand years later have yet to be interpreted.

However, reading that Bru Oengusa is now considered the home of the Grail legend provided a powerful clue and combined with the mythology of the Tuatha de Danaan as the "People of Light," the choices narrowed.

Described as a "passage grave" by modern scholars, the mansion of Angus was more than a burial mound or a mausoleum in ancient Irish myth. It was quite literally a "house" where the dead could live and pass in and out of supernatural reality into this world at will. It was also a place where the living could commune with the spirits of the Otherworld and see, hear and feel the bountiful Grail that awaited them in the spirit-world beyond.

> "And even as he spoke, a light began to glow and to
> pervade the cave, and to obliterate the stone walls and
> the antique hieroglyphics engraven thereon, and to melt

the earthen floor into itself like a fiery sun suddenly
uprisen within the world, and there was everywhere a
wandering ecstacy in the sound: light and sound were
one; light had a voice, and the music hung glittering in
the air ... "A.E. from The Fairy Faith in Celtic Countries
by W.Y. Evans-Wentz

After two hundred years of study Bru Oengusa is now believed to
represent more than just "Irish" or even "Celtic," culture, but a "wide-
ranging pantheon or mythology" that was shared by much of the ancient world. According to Joseph Campbell this solar, quartz clock
built by the mythological Dagda was a primal source for Buddism,
Islam, medieval Christian heresies and eleventh century Crusaders.
It also linked Bru Oengusa to the deepest esoteric secrets of these
religious systems. The Grail had been the object of the occultists
quest for millennia, the divine chalice of "becoming." And as its resting place, Bru Oengusa represented the place where it could be
found; the place where the world of matter ended and the realm of
pure spirit began.

Campbell's statement was a mythological Rosetta Stone tying together a deep vein of consciousness about the origins of spiritual
existence. But it was also an indicator of material existence that pointed
to the egg-shaped mansion of Oengus, where the Dagda—the ancient father/Sun God of the Tuatha De Danaan—had impregnated
matter with the spirit of light and brought forth a race of supernatural
beings that to this day are still regarded as being very much alive.

Whimsical, far fetched?—Not as far as one might think, in fact not
any further than a dream.

ANGUS'S DREAM

One night Oengus [Angus], son of the Dagda dreamt
of the most beautiful girl he had ever seen approached
him. He went to her but she vanished. The same hap-

pened the next night and the next for a whole year so
that Oengus, sick for love of her, began to waste away.
Fingen, the doctor, diagnosed the cause and counselled
that Oengus should ask his mother to scour the countryside for a girl to match his vision, but the year-long search
was in vain. They then consulted Oengus's father, the
Dagda who ruled all the Sidhe-folk in Ireland, and with
the help of King Ailill and Queen Medb dis covered her
to be Caer, the daughter of Ethal Anbual. But Ethal Anbual
refused their summons. And when his palace had been
stormed and Ethal reduced to submission, he declared he
had no power over his daughter Caer, but on the first of
November each year, he said, she changed to a swan at
Loch Bel Dragon, or from a swan to a maiden again.

On the first of November Oengus went to the lake in
the shape of a swan and called to Caer, and she came. He
wrapped himself around her and they flew together to
Bru Oengusa. There they sang an enchanted song that
put people to sleep for three days and three nights and
they stayed together in the house of the Dagda forever.

The idea that human consciousness evolved over the ages from a
fluid-like, dream-state was laid out by Julian James in his book The
Origin of Consciousness in the Breakdown of the Bicameral Mind.
James theorized that early man did not have to sleep to dream, that
reality was plastic, mythic images forming and taking shape alongside
everyday reality in a trance-like state that resembled schizophrenia.
Only when this trance was broken at some point in man's evolution,
perhaps through the Greek development of a mind/body seperation,
did he become "conscious" of the reality he was surrounded by and
begin to establish himself as separate from his dreams.

Another modern scientist, Michael Talbot in his book *The Holographic Universe*, theorized that dreams were a vital part of human

consciousness as well. But given an understanding of quantum physics and the nature of the non-linear universe it tries to portray, Talbot proposed that human consciousness was but an aspect of a larger reality that much resembled a hologram. In a somewhat unsettling notion, Talbot even suggested that in many ways the world of the five senses that we experienced while awake was merely one perspective in a vast array of potential consciousnesses. In that sense, our single perspective dominated by our one personality was actually less real than the dream reality of our sleep, and it was that reality that was actually dreaming of us.

How this actually occurs and what it has to do with our perception of existence, had up until the "age of reason" been the domain of poets. But today, defining "reality" is governed by the realm of physics and it is this realm where we start to look for answers.

According to Fred Allen Wolfe, physicist and author of The Dreaming Universe, physicists attempt to determine what is real by forming a model based on the language of mathematics:

> "Mathematics is just another form of words and images relatable ultimately to scale and number. In physics we ultimately attempt to explain everything in terms of just three basic scales of measurements based on number. These instruments consist of the pendulum, by which we measure time, the balance scale, by which we measure mass; and the straight ruler, by which we measure distance. Through just three concepts, time, mass, and space, we attempt to model everything in the universe."

But Wolfe admits these three measuring sticks are not enough to understand a quantum universe and if science is to accept what it has revealed to itself, a new or perhaps old understanding of this universe is going to have to emerge.

Although Talbot and Wolfe's revelations are in the vanguard of current thinking regarding the quantum nature of existence, the psychological understanding that dreams and consciousness were not all they seemed, did not begin with them. The Psychologist, Carl Jung's entire career was dedicated to an understanding of the dream-realm and to its mythical and what he called archetypal imagery.

In fact the new way of ordering human perception of reality on an omnijective basis was Jung's idea, the core of which he referred to as synchronicity.

In Jung's synchronistic model, the subject/object relationships of Newton's mechanical physics was replaced by an omnijective point of view. Instead of the observable cause and effect relationship where an event is "proven" by its cause, Jung theorized a non-linear world where patterns of events appear but not necessarily in a predictable order or time frame.

Looking back from the future however, the events and the pattern could be clearly seen, suggesting the pattern had been there all along but remained unseen and thus "unproven" to the awake, conscious mind.

In Jung's view, dreaming connected the mind with the omnijective universe, the "trance state" that Julian James theorized.

But how did a mind that had been trained since birth to see the world in the rational, linear terms of Greek philosophers suddenly comprehend beyond its rational senses? How did a mind free itself from the boundaries of height, width, depth and even time and make sense of a vast land of trance?

Since antiquity, secret societies have sought the paths for attaining "higher consciousness" for Western minds. From the mystery rituals of Eleusis, to the tracing boards of Masonry, to the dianetic sciences of L. Ron Hubbard, groups have gathered to recruit, educate and "enlighten" the elect. But through it all, one mind seems to have provided a standard for quantizing the seen and unseen worlds.

It was Pythagoras who attempted to order the Egyptian understanding of soul and spirit by explaining the world through mathematical formulas, explaining all things by their number and conversely, explaining number by the things they represented.

Pythagoras's ordering of the world into Macro-cosm and Micro-cosm was a mathematical schematic of the seen and the unseen world and though many faiths believed in reincarnation, Pathagoras worked out the details in formula. Even the Romans referred to his system, using it to explain the Celts lack of fear for death by saying, "they still hold Pythagoras's belief in the immortality of the soul and rebirth."

Down through the ages, Pythagorean theory played a role in almost every mystical system and even Jung devoted time to studying the Pythagorean "meaning" behind number. Dr. Marie Louise von Franz in her book *Number and Time: Reflections Leading toward a Unification of Depth Psychology and Physics* followed the work of her mentor, (Jung) and explored the concept of number from the viewpoint that it arose as an archtype from the unconscious dream.

Considering that all modern religious systems share many of the same ancient archetypes born of Bru Oengusa and those archetypes are represented by number, it is significant that the number seventeen, the number of minutes the sun impregnates Bru Oengusa at the mid-point of winter should be one of religion's holiest numbers.

The Muslim alchemist Jabir ibn Hayyan, saw the entire material world as based on the number seventeen; consisting of the series 1:3:5:8 which formed the foundation of all other numbers.

Sufis believed the greatest name of God was composed of seventeen letters, while others believed the second coming was to be preceeded by the resurrection of seventeen people each bearing one letter of the name of God. The Great Flood began on the seventeenth day of the second month and ended on the seventeenth day of the seventh month.

Medieval Christian scholars applied the number 17 to the concepts of Law and Grace while Saint Augustine attributed the sum of all the integers between 1 and 17 to the Holy Trinity and the 7 gifts of the spirit.

But what does medieval religious mysticism, Jungian psychology and the coincidence of the timing of light at Bru Oengusa have to do with the flesh and blood of life, and if all material things are reducible to numbers, what does that make us?

Who God is and how God interacts with humanity has been the stuff of religious wars from the beginning of civilization. But the metaphor of God as "light" seems to echo through all religious systems.

Seen in this context the proverbial war of the Light against the Dark takes on new meaning and as we add quantum physics and the Holographic model to the function of light, a new mytho/scientific picture of existence begins to take shape.

THE PEOPLE OF LIGHT

> "And it was to the mansion of Oengus an Broga, that
> Angus brought the body of Diarmid, one of the great
> Irish folk heroes . . . so that he could 'put an aeriel life
> into him so that he will talk to me everyday.'" (Newgrange,
> Archeology, art and legend, by Michael J. O'Kelly)

We can only imagine what the 17 cm. shaft of light fell upon once every winter solstice for all those years that Bru Oegusa lay undisturbed. Not until 1699, when an English landlord named Campbell went looking for stones to mark the boundaries of his land, was the one-ton capstone cracked back and the passage grave invaded. Successive dissections, thefts and desecrations of the now open tomb-space further eroded what secrets Bru Oengusa might have revealed to modern science about Angus's dream-house. But writings do exist of an early investigation by the noted Welsh scholar Edward Lhwyd who was passing through the area at the time.

In a letter dated December 15, 1699 Lhwyd wrote that he had visited the 'cave' which had been opened not too long before and along with the great quantity of bones—stag horns and an "elks head" reported finding "pieces of glass and some kinde of beads."

Human skulls were later found as well, but modern authorities agree that without a definite description of the "glass or beads" it is impossible to say what role such crystals might have played over five-millennia ago as the mid-winter sun reflected through them onto the spiral swirls inside the tomb.

But considering that Bru Oengusa is the egg-shaped house of the Tuatha de Danann, the shape-shifting "People of Light" and that their leader, the Dagda is known in Celtic mythology as the "Sun god," and Otherworld lord, it is not hard to imagine.

According to Celtic legend, Bru Oengusa was a place where the living could talk to the dead, the place where Oengus brought the fallen hero Diarmaid so he could "talk to me everday."

Granted, Oengus is a mythical character to whom supernatural powers were attributed, but even the son of a god needed the power bestowed by the quartz-lined mansion of the Tuatha De Danaan to converse with his dead friend.

Was this ancient power a product of fiction, a fantasy of primitive minds? Or was Bru Oengusa really a "light machine," a form of holographic projector built by a race of advanced minds to materialize spirit into this world?

For most of the last five-thousand years this idea, though not understood in scientific terms, was believed and respected by all the races of the Western world. Even the worldly Romans who came to worship in the first centuries of the Christian era, saw in the Dagda—the creative life-force of the sun—the universal system whereby light is transformed into life.

But with the eighteenth and nineteenth century advance of rationalism, thinking began to change and only now, through the model of advanced holographic technology can our mechanized, rational system of thought begin again to comprehend what the ancients may have known all along.

MYTH, RELIGION AND THE SCIENCE OF LIGHT

If any subject combines mythology, religion and science, it is the subject of light. From the Greek Helios, to the Christian Christ to the modern study of neutrinos, light has always formed the object of our attempts to understand the world we live in.

The workings of light on matter are at the very center of modern physics attempts to define the nature and boundaries of the universe and many physicists have now even come to describe the phenomenon in much the same way that ancient philosophers described it.

Echoing a Mayan expression to explain the importance of neutrinos to matter, Scientific American admitted that "Supernovas are more than distant spectacles; they make and expel the seeds of life." But if matter is "seeded" by neutrinos to form life how does that process effect us, and since we are open to this celestial process, is it not possible that this seeding involves some form of animating spirit as well?

Particle physics is just at the boundaries of understanding the subtle conditions under which light transforms from a wave into a particle of matter and builds life. In fact, in a ghostly hint at what might be the underlying mechanism of creation, Niels Bohr pointed out that subatomic particles only come into existence in the presence of a human observer.

This "observer effect" opens Pandora's box on the story of creation and implies that if something within the human mind is causing reality to take shape, reality is not what it appears to be, and perhaps more importantly, neither is the mind.

Here at the outer limits of Newtonian mechanistic thinking, quantum mechanics and perhaps all of science itself is the essence of the infinitely bendable holographic reality; the realm of the mystic and the world-wide religion once represented by the Bru Oengusa. And it is here, in the study of the unknown and heretofore "unknowable" regions of illumination that we must call on an old model for understanding the universe and our place in it.

> THE MONAD or MONAS "At the dawn of manifesta-
> tion there existed the Divine Monad and none else. The
> Divine Will (Shu, the light) was not projected, neither
> was the material form-nature (Tefnut, the receiver of
> light) made apparent." Dictionary of All Scriptures and
> Myths.

As a model, the concept of the Monad fits a holographic structure of the universe perfectly. At the center of both Celtic and Buddhist thought, the Monad of Form is the symbol of nature, the Tefnut that after taking on arche typal patterns, builds up the forms of existence in the lower planes while the Monad of Life, is Shu, the Spirit of light, the buddhic energy of Truth, Love and Wisdom that projects into the form.

> "The countless monads of form are the specific astro-
> mental molds of every differentiated growth, every vari-
> ety of natural formation on the astral and physical planes.
> These molds have their spiritual prototypes on the higher
> planes, conceived of as schemes of being, germinating
> within and finding expression without in time and space.
> Thus are the atoms guided in the building up of the
> organisms of animals and plants of the present world of
> living things."

According to the Welsh Barddas, "a collection of original documents, illustrative of the theology, wisdom, and usage of the Bardo-Druidic system of the Isle of Britain," the Bardic monad was the key to evolution of the soul.

> The Monad of Form is the sacred vessel, the home

> for the intelligent expression of awareness, like the architecture of a church or a human body. But like all symbols, the Monad of Form is just a receiver for the Monad of Life which . . ."enables it to beget and bring forth its kind."

In the Monad we have the model of ourselves and the world beyond our senses, the union between our constantly evolving human-self and our universal purpose.

But is it a valid model for a materialist scientific civilization based on the perceived permanace of matter and justified by rationalism and reason?

Michael Talbot, author of the Holographic Universe feels certain the Monad is the only model of creation that answers the questions revealed by modern physics while connecting the philosophy of the past with the science of the future.

Citing the seventh-century founder of the Hua-yen school of Buddhist thought, Fa-Tsang, Talbot quotes him as likening the universe to a multi-dimensional network of jewels, each reflecting all the others ad infinitum. And Talbot comes frighteningly close to the actual phenomenon that must have occurred at Bru Oengusa four-thousand years earlier when he states how . . .

> "he [Fa-Tsang] suspended a candle in the middle of a room full of mirrors. This, he told the empress Wu, represented the relationship of the One to the many. Then he took a polished crystal and placed it in the center of the room so that it reflected everything around it. This, he said, showed the relationship of the many to the One."

Talbot then explains how seventeenth-century German mathematician and philosopher Gottfried Leibniz drew on the Hua-yen school of Buddhist thought, proposing that the "crystal" of his experiment was in fact, the monad.

"The universe is constituted out of fundamental enti-
ties he called 'monads,' each of which contains a reflec-
tion of the whole universe."

But even if matter can be produced by a scientist observing it, can light really transform itself through the Monad and assemble into the matter of a human being as the mythology of Bru Oengusa supposes.

Some very knowledgable people once thought this mystery could be solved with the ancient study of alchemy where the spirit was captured and distilled into life through a secret chemical process much as we would do with a photograph.

The process became complete with the manufacture or discovery of the "philosopher's stone," a crystal talisman that would enable the bearer to know all things and achieve a kind of celestial harmony with the cosmos.

Following the first Crusade in 1099 A.D., a small handful of men gathered together the ancient learning of the Middle East and the Orient for the first time in a millennia. At first sanctioned by the religious authorities, the new learning produced by their investigation of the ancient arts produced a spate of mystico-religious practices, that by the Renaissance were drawing the attention of the ecclesiastical authority of Rome.

Called by names such as Rosicrucians, Cabalists, Hermeticists, these students of the Monas or *monastics* sought the answer to the conjuction of spirit and matter. The core of their learning rested on an understanding of the Monad and one of the most famous readings on its function and purpose was even called the Monas Hieroglyphica.

Drawn from European works like Francesco Giorgi's De harmonia mundi, and Cornelius Agrippa's De occulta philosophia, the Monad provided "a double key to the universe," utilizing Pythagorean number theory and Jewish Cabala to unlock the the supercelestial world of angelic spirits and bring them to earth.

Written by Queen Elizabeth I's court magician, John Dee, the

Monas became the bible for the English Reformation and the inspiration for the men of the "Sydney circle," who saw in its "science" the purification of the Christian religion and the beginning of the much awaited Utopian civilization.

For believers like Sydney, whose circle included the illustrious Faerie Queen's Edmund Spencer and the reckless Elizabethan courtier, Walter Raleigh, the attainment of that Utopia for Britain was the single most important event since the birth of Christ.

With Elizabeth I coronated as their divine Monad by virtue of the sacred stone of the Dagda—(the Stone of Scone, said to have been removed from Ireland to Scotland by the Irish Dalriada but then stolen by Edward I)—they believed their magico-chemical process would be complete.

But as the Elizabethan alchemists processed the learning of Dee and the wealth of ancient Egyptian star-magic, which according to British historian Frances Yates, like a hologram relied on "geometry and optics" for its "miraculous effects," they discovered an obstacle.

THE GERALDINES

Long before the "Rosicrucian Enlightenment" or the rise of Renaissance Neo-Platonism, a family of mixed Celtic and Germanic descent had come to Ireland in search of the Dagda's bowl. Bearing the lineage of a Tudor Princess and an ancient quest for the Grail under their dull-black armor they had chosen the Dagda's nickname Crom and the Arabic Abu (son of) as their family motto and settled onto the rich and mystical soil of Southwestern Ireland known as Desmond. There they had re-enacted the ancient ceremony of the hieros gamos, joined in the chemical marriage between heaven and earth—and so prospered from it that by the time of Elizabeth they had literally become a race of their own.

Children of Gerald of Windsor and Nesta, the daughter of Rys ap Tewdr, whose ancestors were said to have included King Arthur, the family had as much claim to the thrown of England as did the Tewdr Henry VIII, and many in Catholic Europe believed more.

According to legend, by coming to Ireland, the Geraldines had joined the household of the Dagda and by embracing the gods and godesses of the Tuatha De Danaan married themselves to the land and the mythologies that made Ireland the home of the Holy Grail.

Today, the meaning and the purpose of that Grail may have been forgotten to the general public. But the quest to find a path through matter and back to the light of conscious understanding continues.

The Grail represents that conscious understanding which has been attained through the soul's process of evolution. This process, contained in the Bardic doctrine of the ancient Celts enables the soul to gradually know itself as the knowledge of physical existence gradually unfolds to it. "Where for the first time exercising freewill in a physical body, it becomes responsible for all its acts. Humanity is a state of liberty, where man can attach himself to either good or evil, as he pleases." (P. 366 Fairy Faith in Celtic Countries by Evans Wentz).